Sheppard Lee

Written by Himself.

(Volume 1)

Robert Montgomery Bird

Alpha Editions

This edition published in 2023

ISBN : 9789357941075

Design and Setting By
Alpha Editions
www.alphaedis.com
Email - info@alphaedis.com

Contents

BOOK I.
CONTAINING INSTRUCTIONS HOW TO
SPEND AND HOW TO RETRIEVE A FORTUNE.

CHAPTER I.

THE AUTHOR'S PREFACE,—WHICH THE READER, IF IN A GREAT HURRY, OR IF IT BE HIS PRACTICE TO READ AGAINST TIME, CAN SKIP.

I have often debated in my mind whether I should give to the world, or for ever lock up within the secrecy of my own breast, the history of the adventures which it has been my lot in life to experience. The importance of any single individual in society, especially one so isolated as myself, is so little, that it can scarcely be supposed that the community at large can be affected by his fortunes, either good or evil, or interested in any way in his fate. Yet it sometimes happens that circumstances conspire to elevate the humblest person from obscurity, and to give the whole world an interest in his affairs; and that man may safely consider himself of some value in his generation, whose history is of a character to instruct the ignorant and inexperienced. Such a man I consider myself to be; and the more I reflect upon my past life, the more I am convinced it contains a lesson which may be studied with profit; while, at the same time, if I am not greatly mistaken, the lesson will be found neither dry nor repulsive, but here and there, on the contrary, quite diverting. The psychologist (I hate big words, but one cannot do without them) and the metaphysician will discover in my relation some new subjects for reflection; and so perhaps will the doctor of medicine and the physiologist: but while I leave these learned gentlemen to discuss what may appear most wonderful in my revealments, I am most anxious that the common reader may weigh the value of what is, at least in appearance, more natural, simple, and comprehensible.

It will be perceived that many of the following adventures are of a truly extraordinary character. There are some men—and to such my story will seem incredible enough—who pride themselves on believing nothing that they do not know, and who endeavour, very absurdly, to restrict the objects of belief to those that admit of personal cognizance. There are others again who boast the same maxim, but have a more liberal understanding of the subjects of knowledge, and permit themselves to believe many things which are susceptible of satisfactory proof, but not of direct cognition. Now I must declare beforehand, in order to avoid all trouble, that, from the very nature of the life I have led, consisting of the strangest transitions and vicissitudes, it is impossible I should have laid up proofs to satisfy any one of the truth of my relation who is disposed to be incredulous. If any one should say, "I doubt," all the answer I could make would be, "Doubt, and be hanged,"—not, however, meaning any offence to anybody; though it is natural one should be displeased at having his veracity questioned. I write for the world at large, which is neither philosophic nor skeptical; and the world will believe me: otherwise it is a less sensible world than I have all along supposed it to be.

CHAPTER II.

THE BIRTH AND FAMILY OF SHEPPARD LEE, WITH SOME ACCOUNT OF HIS TEMPER AND COMPLEXION OF MIND.

I was born somewhere towards the close of the last century,—but, the register-leaf having been torn from the family Bible, and no one remaining who can give me information on the point, I am not certain as to the exact year,—in the State of New-Jersey, in one of the oldest counties that border upon the Delaware river. My father was a farmer in very good circumstances, respectable in his degree, but perhaps more famous for the excellent sausages he used to manufacture for the Philadelphia market, than for any quality of mind or body that can distinguish one man from his fellows. Taking the hint from his success in this article of produce, he gradually converted his whole estate into a market-farm, raising fine fruits and vegetables, and such other articles as are most in demand in a city; in which enterprise he succeeded beyond his highest expectations, and bade fair to be, as in the end he became, a rich man. The only obstacle to a speedy accumulation of riches was a disproportionate increase in the agents of consumption,—his children multiplying on his hands almost as fast as his acres, until he could count eleven in all; a number that filled him at one time with consternation. He used to declare no apple could be expected to ripen on a farm where there were eleven children; and as for watermelons and sugar-corn, it was folly to think of raising them longer. But fate sent my father relief sooner and more effectually than he either expected or desired: nine of the eleven being removed by death in a space of time short of six years. Three (two of whom were twin sisters) were translated in the natural way, falling victims to an epidemic, and were buried in the same grave. A fourth was soon after killed by falling out of an apple-tree. My eldest brother, then a boy of fourteen years old, upon some freak, ran away from home (for he was of a wild, madcap turn), and, getting into an oyster-boat, made a voyage into the bay, where he was lost; for, having fallen overboard, and not being able to swim, a clumsy fellow, who thought to save him in that way, clutched him round the neck with a pair of oyster-tongs, and thereby strangled him. Two others were drowned in a millpond, where they were scraping for snapping-turtles. Another, who was the wag of the family, was killed by attempting to ride a pig, which, running in great alarm through a broken fence into the orchard, dashed his brains out against a white-oak rail; and the ninth died of a sort of hysterical affection, caused by this unlucky exploit of his brother; for he could not cease laughing at it, notwithstanding its melancholy termination, and he died of the fit within twenty-four hours.

Thus, in a few years, there remained but two of all the eleven children,—to wit, my oldest sister Prudence and myself. My mother (from whom I had my Christian name Sheppard, that being her maiden name) died several years before this last catastrophe, her mind having been affected, and indeed distracted, by so many mournful losses occurring in such rapid succession. She fell into a deep melancholy, and died insane.

Being one of the youngest children, I grieved but little for the loss of my brothers and sisters; nor was I able to appreciate the advantage which, in a worldly point of view, their death must prove to me. My father, however, perceived the difference; for, having now so few to look after and be chargeable to him, he could with great propriety consider himself a rich man. He immediately resolved, as I was now his only son, that I should have a good education; and it was not his fault if, in this particular, I fell short of his expectations. I was sent to good schools, and, in course of time, was removed to the college at Nassau Hall, in Princeton, where I remained during three years; that is, until my father's decease; when I yielded to the natural indolence of my temper, and left the college, or rather (for I had formed no resolution on the subject) procrastinated my return from day to day, until it was too late to return.

My natural disposition was placid and easy,—I believe I may say sluggish. I was not wanting in parts, but had as little energy or activity of mind as ever fell to the share of a Jerseyman; and how my father ever came to believe I should make a figure in the world, I cannot conceive, unless it was because he knew he had a fortune to leave me, and saw me safely lodged in a college. It is very certain he encouraged a strong belief that I should one day be a great man; and, I fancy, it was for this reason he showed himself so favourable to me in his will. He left me the bulk of his property, bestowing upon my sister, who had recently married, little beyond a farm which he had purchased in a neighbouring county, but which was a valuable one, and quite satisfied her husband.

But my father was a better judge of sausages than of human character. Besides being deficient, as I humbly confess, in all those qualities that are necessary to the formation of a great man, I had not the slightest desire to be one. Ambition was a passion that never afflicted my mind; and I was so indifferent to the game of greatness which was playing around me, that, I seriously declare, there was a President of the United States elected to office, and turned out again, after having served his regular term, without my knowing any thing about it. I had not even the desire, so common to young men who find themselves in possession of a fortune, to launch out into elegant expenses, to dash about the country with fine horses, servants, and clothes, and to play the spendthrift in cities. On the contrary, I no sooner found myself arrived at my majority, which was a few months after my father's death, than I sat down very quietly on the farm, resolved to take the world easily; which I supposed I might easily do. I had some idea of continuing to conduct the estate, as my father had done before me; but it was a very vague one; and having made one or two efforts to bear myself like a man of business, I soon found the effort was too tiresome for one of my disposition; and I accordingly hired an overseer to manage the property for me.

CHAPTER III.

THE PLEASURES OF HAVING NOTHING TO DO.— SOME THOUGHTS ON MATRIMONY.

Having thus shuffled the cares of business from my shoulders to another's, my time began to weigh a little heavily on my hands, and I cast about for some amusement that might enable me to get rid of it. As there was great abundance of small game, such as quails, partridges, and rabbits, in the neighbourhood, I resolved to turn sportman; and, in consequence, I bought me a dog and gun, and began to harry the country with some spirit. But having the misfortune to shoot my dog the first day, and, soon after, a very valuable imported cow, belonging to a neighbour, for which I was obliged to pay him enormous damages, and meeting besides with but little luck, I grew disgusted with the diversion. My last shot was soon fired; for, having forgotten the provisions of our game-laws, I killed a woodcock too early in the summer, for which, on the information of a fellow who owed me a grudge, I was prosecuted, although it was the only bird I ever killed in all my life, and soundly fined; and this incensed me so much, that I resolved to have nothing more to do with an amusement that cost so much money, and threw me into so many difficulties.

I was then at a loss how to pass my time, until a neighbour, who bred fine horses, persuaded me to buy a pair of blooded colts, and try my luck on the turf; and this employment, though rather too full of cares and troubles to suit me exactly, I followed with no little spirit, and became more proud of my horses than I can well express, until I came to try them on the race-course, where it was my luck, what with stakes and betting together, to lose more money in a single day, than my father had ever made in two years together. I then saw very clearly that horse-racing was nothing better than gambling, and therefore both disreputable and demoralizing; for which reason I instantly gave it up, heartily sick of the losses it had occasioned me.

My overseer, or steward,—for such he may be considered,—whom I always esteemed a very sensible fellow, for he was shrewd and energetic, and at least ten years my senior, then advised me, as I was a young man, with money enough, to travel a little, and see the world: and accordingly I went to New-York, where I was robbed of my luggage and money by a villain whose acquaintance I made in the steamboat, and whom I thought a highly intelligent, gentlemanly personage; though, as it afterward appeared, he was a professor from Sing-Sing, where he had been sawing stone for two years, the governor of New-York having forgiven him, as is the custom, the five other years for which he was committed for, I believe, a fraud committed on his own father.

This loss drove me home again; but being re-encouraged by my overseer, I filled my purse and set out a second time, passing up the Hudson river, with which I was prodigiously pleased, though not with the Overslaugh, where we stuck fast during six hours. I then proceeded to Saratoga, where I remained for two weeks, on account of its being fashionable; but, I declare to Heaven, I was never so tired of any place in my life. I then went to Niagara, which, in spite of the great noise it made, I thought the finest place in the world; and there, I think, I should have continued all summer, had it not been for the crowds of tiresome people that were eternally coming and going, and the great labour of climbing up and down the stairs. However, I was so greatly pleased with what I saw, both at Niagara and along the way, that I should have repeated my travels in after years, as the most agreeable way of passing time, had it not been for the dangers and miseries of such enterprises; for, first, the coaches were perpetually falling over, or sticking in the mud, or jolting over stones, so that one had no security of life or limb; and, secondly, the accommodations at the inns along the road were not to my liking, the food being cooked after the primitive systems of Shem, Ham, and Japheth, and the beds stuck together in the rooms as if for boys at a boarding-school. It is possible that these things are better ordered now; but, from what I have since seen and heard, I am of opinion there is a fine field for cooks, carpenters, and chamber-maids, in the agricultural regions of America. In those days I loved ease and comfort too well to submit to such evils as could be avoided; and, accordingly, after a little experience in the matter, I ceased travelling altogether, the pleasures bearing no sort of proportion to the discomforts.

My time still weighing upon my hands, I was possessed with a sudden idea (which my steward, however, endeavoured to combat), namely, that the tedium of my existence might be dispelled by matrimony; and I resolved to look around me for a wife. After much casting about, I fixed my eyes upon a young lady of the village (for I must inform the reader that my farm was on the skirts of a village, and a very respectable one too, although there were many lazy people in it), who, I thought, was well fitted to make me comfortable; and as she did not seem averse to my first advances, I began to be quite particular, until all the old women in the country declared it was a match, and all the young fellows of my own age, as well as all the girls I knew, became extremely witty at my expense. These things, however, rather encouraged me than otherwise; I believed I was advancing my happiness by the change I contemplated in my condition; and I was just on the point of making formal proposals to the young lady, when an accident set me to considering the enterprise entirely in a new light.

My charmer lived in the house of a married sister, who had a large family of children,—a pack of the most ill-bred imps, I verily believe, that were ever gathered together in any one man's house; but, for politeness' sake, during the first weeks of my courtship, the young sinners were kept out of my way, and, what with cuffing and feeding with sugarplums, were preserved in some sort of order, so that I was not annoyed by them. After a while, however, and when matters had proceeded some length, it was thought unnecessary to treat me longer as a stranger; the children were suffered to take care of themselves; and the consequence was, that, in a short time, I found myself in a kind of Pandemonium whenever I entered the house, with such a whining, and squeaking, and tumbling, and bawling, and fighting among the young ones, as greatly discomposed my nerves; and, to make the matter worse, the mother made no difficulty at times, when the squabbling grew to a height, of taking a switch to one, and boxing the ears of another, and scolding roundly at a third, to reduce them to order; and all this in my presence, and under the nose of my charmer.

I began to fancy the married life could not be altogether so agreeable as I had pictured it to my imagination; and in this belief I was confirmed by a visit to my sister, who had three children of her own, all of whom, as I now perceived (for I had not noticed it before, having no particular inducement to make me observant), were given to squabbling and bawling, just like other children, while my sister did her share of boxing and scolding. I thought to myself, "What should *I* do with a dozen children squeaking all day and night in my house, and a scolding wife dragooning them into submission?"

The thought disconcerted me, and the fear of such a consummation greatly chilled the ardour of my affection; so that the young lady, observing my backwardness, and taking offence at it, cast her eyes upon another wooer who had made her an offer, and, to my great satisfaction, married him on the spot.

I was never more relieved in my life, and I resolved to reflect longer upon the subject before making advances of that nature a second time. My overseer, who had from the first (for I made him my confidant) been opposed to the match, on the ground that I ought to enjoy my liberty, at least until I was thirty, was greatly rejoiced at the rupture, and swore that I had made a lucky escape; for he had always thought, in his own mind, that the lady was at bottom, though she concealed it from me, a Tartar and fire-eater. In this, however, he was mistaken; for, from all I have heard of her since, she has proved a most amiable and sweet-tempered woman, and her husband is said to be very happy with her.

CHAPTER IV.

HOW TO CONDUCT A FARM TO THE BEST ADVANTAGE, AND STEER CLEAR OF THE LAWYERS.

It is not my intention to dwell longer upon the history of this period of my life, nor to recount in detail how my easy and indolent temper at last proved the ruin of me. I gave myself up to laziness, neglecting my affairs to such a degree that they soon became seriously entangled; and, to make a long story short, I found myself, before I had completed my twenty-eighth year, reduced from independence, and almost affluence, to a condition bordering upon actual poverty. My farm, under the management of Mr. Aikin Jones (for that was my steward's name), went gradually to ruin; my orchards rotted away, without being replanted; my meadows were converted into swamps; my corn-fields filled with gullies; my improvements fell into decay; and my receipts began to run short of my expenses. Then came borrowing and mortgaging, and, by-and-by, the sale of *this* piece of land to remove the encumbrance upon *that*; until I suddenly found myself in the condition of my father when he began the world; that is to say, the master of a little farm of forty acres,—the centre and nucleus of the fifteen hundred which he had got possession of and bequeathed to me, but which had so soon slipped through my fingers. There was this difference, however, between us; the land, when my father obtained it, was in good condition; it was now (so well had it prospered under Jones's hands) entirely worn out and empoverished, and not worth a fourth part of its original value.

To add to my chagrin, I discovered that Mr. Aikin Jones, whom I had treated rather as a friend than servant, had abused my confidence; in other words, that he was a rogue and villain, who had taken advantage of my disinclination to business, and my ignorance, as I believe I must call it, to swindle me out of my property, which he had the best opportunities to do. Whether he effected his purpose by employing my own funds or not, I cannot say; but, it is very certain, all the different mortgages in which I was entangled came, some how or other, by hook and by crook, into his hands, and he took care to make the best use of them. In a word, Mr. Jones became a rich man, and I a poor one; and I had the satisfaction, every day when I took a walk over my forty-acre farm, as the place was familiarly called, though the true name was Watermelon Hill, to find myself stopped, which way soever I directed my steps, by the possessions of Mr. Aikin

Jones, my old friend and overseer, whom I often saw roll by in his carriage, while I was trudging along through the mud.

At the same time that I met with this heavy misfortune, I had to endure others that were vexatious enough. My brother-in-law and sister had their suspicions of Mr. Jones, and often cautioned me against him, though in vain,—not that I had any very superstitious reliance on the gentleman's integrity, but because I could not endure the trouble of examining into his proceedings and accounts, and chose therefore to believe him honest. This, and my general indolence and indifference to my affairs, incensed them both to that degree, that my sister did not scruple to tell me to my face that I had lost all the little sense I ever possessed; while my brother-in-law took the freedom of saying of me in public, "that I was *wrong* in the upper story,"—in other words, that I was mad; and he had the insolence to hint "that it ran in my blood,—that I had inherited it from my mother," she, as I mentioned before, having lost her mind before her decease. I was so much irritated by these insults on their part, that I quarrelled with them both, though by no means of a testy or choleric disposition; and it was many years before we were reconciled. Having therefore neither friends nor family, I was left to bear my misfortunes alone; which was a great aggravation of them all.

CHAPTER V.

THE AUTHOR FINDS HIMSELF IN TROUBLE.—SOME ACCOUNT OF HIS SERVANT, HONEST JAMES JUMBLE.

I have always described myself as of an easy, contented disposition; and such I was born. But misfortune produces sad changes in our tempers, as it was soon my lot to experience. Before, however, I describe the change that took place in mine, it is fit I should let the reader understand to what condition I was reduced by the perfidy of Jones,—or, as I should rather say, by my own culpable neglect of my affairs.

My whole landed possessions consisted of a farm of forty acres, which I had, after the fashion of some of my richer neighbours in other states, suffered to fall into the most wretched condition imaginable. My meadow-lands, being broken in upon by the river, and neglected, were converted into quagmires, reed-brakes, and cat-tail patches, the only use of which was to shelter wild-fowl and mire cattle. However, my live-stock was scanty enough, and the only sufferers were my neighbours, whose cows easily made their way through my fences, and stuck fast in the mud at their pleasure. My fields were overgrown here with mullein and St. John's-wort, and there with sand-burs and poke-berries. My orchards were in an equally miserable condition,—the trees being old, rotten, or worm-eaten, half of them torn down by the winds, and the remainder fit for nothing but fire-wood. My barn was almost roofless; and as for a stable, I had so little occasion for one, that my old negro-man Jim, of whom I shall have more to say hereafter, or his wife Dinah, or both together, thinking they could do nothing better with it, helped the winds to tear it to pieces, especially in the winter, when it formed a very convenient wood-pile. My dwelling-house was also suffering from decay. It was originally a small frame building; but my father had added to it one portion after another, until it became spacious; and the large porches in front and on the rear, gave it quite a genteel, janty air. But this it could not long keep; the sun and rain gradually drove the white paint from the exterior, and the damps getting inside, the fine paper-hangings, pied and spotted, peeled from the walls. The window-frames rotted, and the glasses left them one after another; and one day in a storm one half the front porch tumbled down, and the remainder, which I propped up as well as I could, had a mighty mean and poverty-stricken appearance. The same high wind carried away one of my chimneys, which, falling on a corner of the roof, crushed that into the garret, and left one whole gable-end in ruins.

It must not be supposed that my property presented altogether this wretched appearance at the moment of my losses. It was in truth bad enough then; but I am now describing it as it appeared some few years after, when my miseries were accumulated in the greatest number, and I was just as poor as I could be.

In all this period of trouble and vexation I had but one friend, if I dare call him such; though I should have been glad half the time to be rid of him. This was my negro-man Jim, or Jim Jumble, as he was called, of whom I spoke before,—an old fellow that had been a slave of my father, and was left to me in his will. He was a crabbed, self-willed old fellow, whom I could never manage, but who would have all things his own way, in spite of me. As I had some scruples of conscience about holding a slave, and thought him of no value whatever, but, on the contrary, a great trouble, I resolved to set him free, and accordingly mentioned my design to him; when, to my surprise, he burst into a passion, swore he would *not* be free, and told me flatly I was his master, and I should take care of him: and the absurd old fool ended by declaring, if I made him a free man he would have the law of me, "he would, by ge-hosh!"

I never could well understand the cause of his extreme aversion to being made free; but I suppose, having got the upper hand of me, and being wise enough to perceive the difference between living, on the one hand, a lazy life, without any care whatever, as my slave, and, on the other, labouring hard to obtain a precarious subsistence as a free man, he was determined to stick by me to the last, whether I would or not. Some little affection for me, as I had grown up from a boy, as it were, under his own eye, was perhaps at the bottom of his resolution; but if there were, it was of a strange quality, as he did nothing but scold and grumble at me all day long. I remember, in particular, that, when the match I spoke of before was broken off, and he had heard of it, he came to me in a great passion, and insolently asked "what I meant by courting a wife, who would be a good mistress to him, and not marrying her?" and, on my condescending to explain the reasons of my change of mind, he told me plumply, "I had no more sense than a nigger; for women was women, and children children; and he was tired living so long in a house with none but me and Massa Jones for company."

I suppose it was old Jim's despair of my ever marrying, that put him upon taking a wife himself; for one day, not long after I was reduced to the forty-acre farm, he brought home a great ugly free negro-woman, named Dinah, whom he installed into the kitchen without the least ceremony, and without so much as even informing me of his intention. Having observed her two or three times, and seeing her at last come bouncing into the dinner-room to wait on me, I asked her who she was, and what she wanted; to which she answered, "she was Jim's wife, and Jim had sent her in to take care of me."

It was in this way the old rascal used me. It was in vain to complain; he gave me to understand in his own language, "He knew what was what, and there was no possuming an old nigger like him; and if I had made *him* overseer, instead of Massa Jones, it would have been all the better for me."

And, in truth, I believe it would; for Jim would never have cheated me, except on a small scale; and if he had done no work himself, it is very certain he would have made everybody else work; for he was a hard master when he had anybody under him.

I may here observe, and I will do the old fellow the justice to confess, that I found him exceedingly useful during all my difficulties. What labour was bestowed upon the farm, was bestowed almost altogether by him and his wife Dinah. It is true he did just what he liked, and without consulting me,—planting and harvesting, and even selling what he raised, as if he were the master and owner of all things, and laying out what money he obtained by the sales, just as his own wisdom prompted; and finding I could do nothing better, I even let him have his own way; and it was perhaps to my advantage that I did.

But I grew poorer and poorer, notwithstanding: and at that period, which I shall ever be inclined to consider as the true beginning of my eventful life, I was reduced almost to the point of despair; for my necessities had compelled me to mortgage the few miserable acres I had left, and I saw nothing but utter ruin staring me in the face.

CHAPTER VI.

SHEPPARD LEE EXPERIENCES HIS SHARE OF THE RESPECT THAT IS ACCORDED TO "HONEST POVERTY."—HIS INGENIOUS AND HIGHLY ORIGINAL DEVICES TO AMEND HIS FORTUNE.

It may be asked, why I made no efforts to retrieve my fortunes? I answer to that, that I made many, but was so infatuated that I never once thought of resorting to the most obvious, rational, and only means; that is to say, of cultivating with industry my forty acres, as my father had done before me. This idea, so sluggish was my mind, or so confused by its distresses, never once occurred to me; or if it did, it presented so many dreary images, and so long a prospect of dull and disagreeable labour, that I had not the spirit to pursue it. The little toil I was forced to endure—for my necessities now compelled me at times to work with my own hands—appeared to me intolerably irksome; and I was glad to attempt any thing else that seemed to promise me good luck, and did not require positive labour.

The first plan of bettering my fortune that I conceived, was to buy some chances in a lottery, which I thought an easy way of making money; as indeed it is, when a man can make any. I had my trouble for my pains, with just as many blanks as I had bought tickets; upon which I began to see clearly that adventuring in a lottery was nothing short of gambling, as it really is; and so I quitted it.

I then resolved to imitate the example of a neighbour, who had made a great sum of money by buying and selling to advantage stock in a southern gold-mining company; and being very sanguine of success, I devoted all the money I could scrape together to the purpose, and that so wisely, that a second instalment being suddenly demanded, I had nothing left to discharge it with, and no means of raising any; the consequence of which was, that I was forced to sell at the worst time in the world, and retired from the concern with just one fifth the sum I had invested in it. I saw then that I had no talent for speculating, and I began to have my doubts whether stock-jobbing was not just as clear gambling as horse-racing and lottery speculation.

I tried some ten or a dozen other projects with a view to better my condition; but, as I came off with the same luck from all, I do not think it necessary to mention them. I will, however, state, as a proof how much my difficulties had changed my mind on that subject, that one of them was of a matrimonial character. My horror of squabbling children and scolding wives melted away before the prospect of sheriffs and executions; and there being a rich widow in the neighbourhood, I bought me a new coat, and made her a declaration. But it was too late in the day for me, as I soon discovered; for besides giving me a flat refusal, she made a point of revealing the matter to all her acquaintance, who did nothing but hold me up to ridicule.

I found that my affairs were falling into a desperate condition; and not knowing what else to do, I resolved to turn politician, with the hope of getting some office or other that might afford me a comfortable subsistence.

This was the maddest project that ever possessed my brain; but it was some time before I came to that conclusion. But, in truth, from having been the easiest and calmest tempered man in the world, I was now become the most restless and discontented, and incapable of judging what was wise and what foolish. I reflected one day, that of my old school and college mates who were still alive, there was not one who had not made some advance in the world, while I had done nothing but slip backwards. It was the same thing with dozens of people whom I remembered as poor farmers' boys, with none of the advantages I had possessed, but who had outstripped me in the road to fortune, some being now rich cultivators, some wealthy manufacturers and merchants, while two or three had got into the legislature, and were made much of in the newspapers. One of my old companions had emigrated to the Mississippi, where he was now a cotton-planter, with a yearly revenue of twenty or thirty thousand dollars; another had become a great lawyer in an adjacent state; and a third, whom I always thought a very shallow, ignorant fellow, and who was as poor as a rat to boot, had turned doctor, settled down in the village, and, besides getting a great practice, had married the richest and finest girl in all the county. There was no end to the number of my old acquaintances who had grown wealthy and distinguished; and the more I thought of them, the more discontented I became.

My dissatisfaction was increased by discovering with what little respect I was held among these happy people. The doctor used to treat me with a jocular sort of familiarity, which I felt to be insulting; the lawyer, who had eaten many a dinner at my table, when I was able to invite him, began to make me low bows, instead of shaking hands with me; and the cotton-planter, who had been my intimate friend at college, coming to the village on a visit to his relations, stared me fiercely in the face when I approached him, and with a lordly "hum—ha!" asked me "Who the devil I might be?" As for the others, they treated me with as little consideration; and I began to perceive very plainly that I had got into the criminal stage of poverty, for all men were resolved to punish me. It is no wonder that poverty is the father of crime, since the poor man sees himself treated on all hands as a culprit.

I had never before envied a man for enjoying more consideration in the world than myself: but the discovery that I was looked upon with contempt filled me with a new subject for discontent. I envied my richer neighbours not only for being rich, but for being what they considered themselves, my superiors in standing. I may truly say, I scarce ever saw, in those days, a man with a good coat on his back, without having a great desire to beat him. But as I was a peaceable man, my anger never betrayed me into violence.

CHAPTER VII.

THE AUTHOR BECOMES A POLITICIAN, AND SEEKS FOR AN OFFICE.—THE RESULT OF THAT PROJECT.

My essay in politics was soon made. I spent a whole week in finding out who were the principal office-holders, candidates, and busybodies, both in the state and the general governments; and which were the principal parties; there being so many, that an honest man might easily make a mistake among them. Being satisfied on these points, I chose the strongest party, on the principle that the majority must always be right, and attended the first public meeting that was held, where I clapped my hands and applauded the speeches with so much spirit, that I was taken notice of and highly commended by several of the principal leaders. In truth, I pleased them so well, that they visited me at my house, and encouraged me to take a more prominent part in the business of politics; and this I did, for at the next meeting, I got up and made a speech; but what it was about I know no more than the man in the moon, otherwise I would inform the reader. My only recollection of it is, that there was great slashing at the banks and aristocrats that ground the faces of the poor; for I was on what our opponents called the hurrah side, and these were the things we talked about. I received uncommon applause; and, in fact, there was such a shouting and clapping of hands, that I was obliged to put an end to my discourse sooner than I intended.

But I found myself in great favour with the party, and being advised by the leaders, who considered I had a talent that way, to set about converting all I knew in the county who were not of our party, and they hinting that I should certainly, in case the county was gained (for our county happened to be a little doubtful at that time), be appointed to the postoffice in the village, I mounted my old horse Julius Cesar, and set out with greater zeal than I had ever shown in my life before. I visited everybody that I knew, and a great many that I did not know; and, wherever I went, I held arguments, and made speeches, with a degree of industry that surprised myself, for certainly I was never industrious before. It is certain, also, that there was never a labourer in the field of politics that better deserved his reward,— never a soldier of the party ranks that had won a better right to a share in the spoils of victory. I do not pretend to say, indeed, that I converted anybody to our belief; for all seemed to have made up their minds beforehand; and I never yet knew or heard of a man that could be argued out of his politics, who had once made up his mind on the subject. I laboured, however, and that with astonishing zeal; and as I paid my own expenses, and treated all thirsty souls that seemed approachable in that way to good liquor, I paid a good round sum, that I could ill spare, for the privilege of electioneering; and was therefore satisfied that my claim to office would hold good.

And so it did, as was universally allowed by all the party; but the conviction of its justice was all I ever gained in reward of my exertions. The battle was fought and won, the party was triumphant, and I was just rejoicing in the successful termination of my hopes, when they were blasted by the sudden appointment of another to the very office which I considered my own. That other was one of the aforesaid leaders, who had been foremost in commending my zeal and talents, and in assuring me that the office should be mine.

I was confounded, petrified, enraged; the duplicity and perfidy of my new friends filled me with indignation. It was evident they must all have joined in recommending my rival to the office; for he was a man of bad character, who must, without such recommendations, have missed his aim. All therefore had recommended him, and all had promised their suffrages to me! "The scoundrels!" said I to myself. I perceived that I had fallen among thieves; it was clear that no party could be in the right, which was led by such unprincipled men; there was corruption at the heart of the whole body; the party consisted of rogues who were gaping after the loaves and fishes; their honesty was a song—their patriotism a farce. In a word, I found I had joined the wrong party, and I resolved to go over to the other, sincerely repenting the delusion that had made me so long the advocate of wrong and deception.

But fortune willed otherwise. I had arrived at the crisis of my fate; and before I could put my purpose into execution, I was suddenly involved in that tissue of adventure, which, I have no doubt, will be considered the most remarkable that ever befell a human being.

CHAPTER VIII.

A DESCRIPTION OF THE OWL-ROOST, WITH MR. JUMBLE'S IDEAS IN RELATION TO CAPTAIN KID'S MONEY.

———

For five mortal days I remained at home, chewing the bone of reflection; and a hard bone it was. On the sixth there came a villanous constable with a—the reader may suppose what. I struck a bargain with him, and he took his leave, and Julius Cesar also, saddle, bridle, and all; whereby I escaped an introduction to the nearest justice of the peace. The next visit, I had good reason to apprehend, would be from the sheriff; for, having failed to pay up the interest on the mortgage, the mortgagee had discoursed, and that in no very mysterious strain, on the virtues of a writ of *Venditioni Exponas*, or some other absurd and scoundrelly invention of the lawyers. I was at my wits' end, and I wished that I was a dog; in which case I should have gone mad, and bitten the new post-master and all his friends.

"Very well," said I to myself; "the forty-acre is no longer mine." I clapped on my hat, and walked into the open air, resolved to take a look at it before the sheriff came to convince me it belonged to some other person. As I passed from the door, I looked up to the broken porch: "May it fall on the head of my successor," I said.

It was a summer eve,—a day in July; but a raw wind blew from the northeast, and the air was as chill as in November. I buttoned my coat, and as I did so, took a peep at my elbows: I required no second look to convince me that I was a poor man.

The ruined meadows of which I have spoken, lie on a little creek that makes in from the Delaware. Their shape is the worst in the world, being that of a triangle, the longest leg of which lies on the water. Hence the expense of embanking them is formidable,—a circumstance for which the muskrats have no consideration. The apex of the angle is a bog, lying betwixt two low hillocks, or swells of ground, between which crawls a brook, scarce deep enough to swim a tadpole, though an ox may hide in the mud at the bottom. It oozes from a turfy ledge or bar, a few feet higher than the general level of the hollow, which terminates above it in a circular basin of two acres in area. This circular basin is verdant enough to the eye, the whole surface being covered by a thick growth of alders, arrow-wood, water-laurels, and other shrubs that flourish in a swamp, as well as a bountiful sprinkling of cat-tails on the edges. The soil is a vegetable jelly;

and how any plant of a pound in weight could ever sustain itself on it, I never was able to comprehend. It is thought to be the nearest road to the heart of the Chinese empire; to find which, all that is necessary to do is, to take a plunge into it head foremost, and keep on until you arrive at daylight among the antipodes.

The whole place has a solitary and mournful appearance, which is to many made still more dreary and even sepulchral by the appearance of a little old church, built by the Swedes many a year ago, but now in ruins, and the graveyard around it, these being but a short distance off, and on the east side of the hollow. The spot is remote from my dwelling, and apparently from all others; nevertheless there is a small farmhouse—it was once mine—on a by-road, not many rods from the old church. A path, not often trodden, leads from my house to the by-road, and crosses the hollow by the grassy ledge spoken of before. It is the shortest path to the village, and I sometimes pursued it when walking thither.

This lonesome spot had a very bad name in our neighbourhood, and was considered to be haunted. Its common name was the Owl-roost, given it in consequence of the vast numbers of these birds that perched, and I believe nested in the centre of the swamp, where was a place comparatively dry, or supposed to be so, for I believe no one ever visited it, and a clump of trees larger than those in other places. Some called the place Captain Kid's Hole, after that famous pirate who was supposed to have buried his money there, as he is supposed to have buried it in a hundred thousand other dismal spots along the different rivers of America. Old Jim Jumble was a devout believer in the story, and often tried his luck in digging for the money, but without success; which he attributed to the circumstance of his digging in the daytime, whereas midnight was, in his opinion, the only true time to delve for charmed treasure. But midnight was the period when the ghosts came down from the old graveyard to squeak about the swamp; and I never heard of Jim being found in that neighbourhood after nightfall. The truth is, the owls never hear any one go by after dark without saluting him with a horrible chorus of hooting and screeching, that will make a man's hair rise on his head; and I have been sometimes daunted by them myself.

To this place I directed my steps; and being very melancholy, I sat down at the foot of a beech-tree that grew near the path. I thought of the owls, and the ghosts, and of Captain Kid into the bargain, and I marvelled to myself whether there could be any foundation for the belief that converted such nooks into hiding-places for his ill-gotten gold. While I thought over the matter, I began to wish the thing could be true, and that some good spirit might direct me to the spot where the money lay hid; for, sure enough, no one in the world had greater necessity for it than I. I conned over the many stories that old Jim had told me about the matter, as well as all the nonsensical ceremonies that were to be performed, and the divers ridiculous dangers to be encountered by those who sought the treasure; all which were mere notions that had entered his absurd head, but which he had pondered over so often and long, that he believed they had been told him by others.

The great difficulty, according to his belief, and a necessary preliminary to all successful operations, was first to discover exactly the spot where the treasure lay buried; and, indeed, this seemed to be a very needful preliminary. The discovery was to be made only by dreaming of the spot three nights in succession. As to dreaming twice, that was nothing: Jim had twenty times dreamed two nights together that he had fallen upon the spot; but upon digging it discovered nothing. Having been so lucky as to dream of a place three successive nights, then the proper way to secure the treasure, as he told me, would be, to select a night when the moon was at the full, and begin digging precisely at twelve o'clock, saying the Lord's prayer backwards all the time, till the money was found. And here lay the danger; a single blunder in the prayer, and wo betide the devotee! for the devil, who would be standing by all the time, would that moment pounce upon his soul, and carry it away in a flame of brimstone.

CHAPTER IX.

SHEPPARD LEE STUMBLES UPON A HAPPY MAN, AND QUARRELS WITH HIM.

While I sat pondering over these matters, and wondering whether *I* could say the prayer backwards, and doubting (for, to my shame be it spoken, I had not often, of late years, said it *forward*), I heard a gun go off in the meadow; and rising, and walking that way, I discovered a sportsman who had just shot a woodcock, which his dog carried to him in his mouth. I knew the gunner at first sight to be a gentleman of Philadelphia, by the name of Higginson, a brewer, who was reputed to be very wealthy, and who had several times before visited our neighbourhood, for the purpose of shooting. I knew little of him except his name, having never spoken to him. The neighbours usually addressed him as squire, though I knew not for what reason. He was a man of forty or forty-five years old, somewhat fat and portly, but with a rosy, hearty complexion, looking the very personification of health and content; and, indeed, as I gazed at him, strolling up and down with his dog and gun, I thought I had never before seen such a picture of happiness.

But the sight only filled me with gloom and anger. "Here," said I to myself, "is a man rich and prosperous, who passes his whole life in an amusement that delights him, goes whither he likes, does what he will, eats, drinks, and is merry, and the people call him squire wherever he goes. I wish I were he; for, surely, he is the happiest man in the world!"

While I pondered thus, regarding him with admiration and hatred together, a bird rose at his feet, and he shot it; and the next moment another, which he served in the same way.

I noted the exultation expressed in his countenance, and I was filled with a sudden fury. I strode up to him while he was recharging his piece, and as I approached him, he looked up and gave me a nod of so much complacency and condescension together, that it rendered me ten times madder than ever.

"Sir," said I, looking him full in the face, "before you shoot any more birds here, answer me a question. Who do you go for—the Administration, or the Opposition?"

This was a very absurd way of beginning a conversation with a stranger; but I was in such a fury I scarce knew what I said. He gave me a stare, and then a smile, and nodding his head good-humouredly, replied,

"Oh! for the Administration, to be sure!"

"You do, sir!" I rejoined, shaking my fist at him. "Then, sir, let me tell you, sir, you belong to a scoundrelly party, and are a scoundrel yourself, sir: and so, sir, walk off my place, or I'll prosecute you for a trespass."

"You insolent ragamuffin!" said he.

Ragamuffin! Was I sunk so low that a man trespassing on my own property could call me ragamuffin?

"You poor, miserable shote!"—

So degraded that I could be called a pig?

"You half-starved old sand-field Jersey kill-deer!"—

A Jersey kill-deer!

"You vagabond! You beggar! You Dicky Dout!"—

I was struck dumb by the multitude and intensity of his epithets; and before I could recover speech, he shouldered his gun, snapped his fingers in my face, and whistling to his dog, walked off the ground. Before he had gone six steps, however, he turned round, gave me a hard look, and bursting into a laugh, exclaimed, tapping his forehead as he spoke,—

"Poor fellow! you're wrong in your upper story!"

With that he resumed the path, and crossed over to the old church, where I lost sight of him.

"Wrong in my upper story!" It was the very phrase which Tom Alderwood, my brother-in-law, had applied to me, and which had given me such mortal offence that I had never forgiven him, and had refused to be reconciled, even when, as my difficulties began to thicken about me, he came to offer me his assistance. "Wrong in my upper story!" I was so much confounded by the man's insolence, that I remained rooted to the spot until he had got out of sight; and then, not knowing what else to do, I returned home; when I had a visit from old Jim, who entered the apartment, and not knowing I had sold my horse, cried out, "Massa Sheppard, want money to shoe Julius Cesar 'morrow morning. Blacksmith swear no trust no more."

"Go to the devil, you old rascal!" said I, in a rage.

"Guess I will," said Jim, shaking his head: "follow hard after massa."

That insinuation, which struck me as being highly appropriate, was all I got for supper; for it was Jim's way, when I offended him of an afternoon, to sneak off, taking Dinah with him, and thus leave me to shift for myself during the whole night as I could. There was never a more tyrannical old rascal than Jim Jumble.

CHAPTER X.

SHEPPARD LEE HAS AN EXTRAORDINARY DREAM, WHICH PROMISES TO BE MORE ADVANTAGEOUS THAN ANY OF HIS PREVIOUS ONES.

———

I went therefore supperless to bed; but I dreamed of Captain Kid's money, and the character of my dream was quite surprising. I thought that my house had fallen down in a high wind, as, indeed, it was like enough to do, and that I was sitting on a broken chair before the ruins, when Squire Higginson made his appearance, looking, however, like a dead man; for his face was pale, and he was swathed about with a winding-sheet. Instead of a gun he carried a spade in his hand; and a great black pig followed at his heels in place of his dog. He came directly towards me, and looking me full in the face, said, "Sheppard Lee, what are you doing here?" but I was struck with fear, and could make no reply. With that, he spoke again, saying, "The sheriff is coming to levy on your property; get up, therefore, and follow me." So saying, he began to walk away, whistling to the pig, which ran at his heels like a dog; and I found myself impelled to follow him. He took the path to the Owl-roost, and, arriving there, came to a pause, saying, "Sheppard Lee, you are a poor man, and eaten up with discontent; but I am your friend, and you shall have all your wishes." He then turned to the pig, which was rooting under a gum-tree, and blowing his whistle, said, "Black Pig, show me some game, or I'll trounce you;" and immediately the pig began to run about snuffing, and snorting, and coursing like a dog, so that it was wonderful to behold him. At last the squire, growing impatient, and finding fault with the animal's ill success, for he discovered nothing, took a whip from under his shroud, and fell to beating him; after which the pig hunted more to his liking; and, having coursed about us for a while, ran up to the beech-tree, under which I had sat the day before, and began with snout and hoof to tear up the earth at its roots. "Oho!" said Squire Higginson, "I never knew Black Pig to deceive me. We shall have fine sport now." Then, putting the spade into my hands, he bade me dig, exhorting me to be of good heart, for I was now to live a new life altogether. But before I struck the spade into the earth he drew a mark on the ground, to guide me, and the figure was precisely that of a human grave. Not daunted by this circumstance, for in my dream it appeared natural enough, I began to dig; and after throwing out the earth to a depth just equal to the length of the spade, I discovered an iron coffin, the lid of which was in three pieces, and, not being fastened in any way, was therefore easily removed.

Judge of my transports when, having lifted up the piece in the middle, I found the whole coffin full of gold and silver, some in the form of ancient coins, but the most of it in bars and ingots. I would have lifted up the whole coffin, and carried it away at once, but that was impossible; I therefore began to fill my pockets, my hat, my handkerchief, and even my bosom; until the squire bade me cease, telling me I should visit the treasure at the same hour on the following night. I then replaced the iron cover, and threw the earth again into the grave, as the squire commanded; and then leaving him, and running home as hard as I could, in fear lest some one should see me, I fell into a miry place, where I was weighed down by the mass of gold I had about me, and smothered. In the midst of my dying agonies I awoke, and found that all was a dream.

Ah! how much torment a poor man has dreaming of riches! The dream made me very melancholy; and I went moping about all that day, wishing myself anybody or any thing but that I was, and hiding in the woods at the sight of any one who chanced to pass by, for I thought everybody was the sheriff. I went to bed the following night in great disorder of spirit, and had no sooner closed my eyes than I dreamed the same dream over again. The squire made his appearance as before, led me to the Owl-roost, and set the black pig hunting until the grave was found. In a word, the dream did not vary in a single particular from that I had had the night before; and when I woke up the next day, the surprise of such an occurrence filled me with new and superstitious ideas, and I awaited the next night with anxious expectations, resolved, if the dream should be repeated again, to go dig at the place, and see what should come of it.

Remembering what old Jim had said in regard to the full of the moon, I went to a neighbour's to look at his almanack (for I had none of my own), and discovered, to my unspeakable surprise and agitation, though I had half known it before, that the moon we then had would be at her full between ten and eleven o'clock on the following morning.

Such a coincidence betwixt the time of my dreams and the proper period for hunting the treasure (since at the full moon was the proper time), was enough of itself to excite my expectations; and the identity between the two visions was so extraordinary, that I began to believe that the treasure did really exist in the Owl-roost, which, being very solitary, and yet conveniently accessible from the river through the medium of the creek, was one of the best hiding-places in the world, and that I was the happy man destined to obtain it.

I went to bed accordingly the third night with a strong persuasion that the vision would be repeated: I was not disappointed. I found myself again digging at the beech-roots, and scraping up great wedges of gold and silver from the iron coffin. What was remarkable in this dream, however, was, that when I had picked up as much as I could carry, the squire nodded to me, and said, "Now, Sheppard Lee, you know the way to Captain Kid's treasure, and you can come to-morrow night by yourself." And what was further observable, I did not dream of falling into a miry place on this occasion, but arrived safely home, and beheld with surprise and delight that my house, which I had left in ruins, was standing up more beautiful than ever it had been, newly painted from top to bottom, and the pillars of the porch were gilded over, and shining like gold.

While enjoying this agreeable prospect I awoke, and such was the influence of the vision on my mind, and the certain belief I now cherished that the vast treasure was mine,—a whole coffinful of gold and silver,—that I fell to shouting and dancing; so that old Jim Jumble, who ran up into my chamber to see what was the matter, was persuaded I had gone mad, and began to blubber and scold, and take on in the most diverting way in the world.

I pacified him as well as I could, but resolved to keep my secret until I could surprise him with the sight of my treasure, all collected together in the house; and I proceeded without delay to make such preparations as were proper for the coming occasion. I took a spade and mattock, and carried them to the hollow, where I hid them among the bushes. But this I found difficult to do as secretly as I wished; for old Jim, either from suspecting what I was after, or believing I had lost my mind, kept dogging me about; so that it was near midday before I succeeded in giving him the slip, and carrying my tools to the hollow.

CHAPTER XI.

IN WHICH THE READER IS INTRODUCED TO A PERSONAGE WHO MAY CLAIM HIS ACQUAINTANCE HEREAFTER.

In this place, to my dismay, I stumbled upon a man, who, from the character he had in the neighbourhood, I was afraid was hunting the treasure, as well as myself. He was an old German doctor, called Feuerteufel, which extraordinary name, as I had been told, signified, in German, *Fire-devil*. He had come to our village about two weeks before, and nobody knew for what reason. All day long he wandered about among the woods, swamps, and marshes, collecting plants and weeds, stones, animals, and snakes, which he seemed to value very highly. Some thought he was a counterfeiter in disguise, and others called him a conjurer. Many were of opinion he was hunting for gold-mines, or precious stones; while others had their thoughts, and said he was the devil, his appearance being somewhat grim and forbidding. As for myself, having lighted upon him once or twice in the woods, I did not know what to think of him; but I did not like his looks. He was very tall and rawboned, with long arms, and immense big hands; his skin was extremely dark and pock-marked, and he had a mouth that ran from ear to ear, and long, bushy, black hair. His eyes were like saucers, and deep sunk in their sockets, with tremendous big black eyebrows ever frowning above them; and what made him look remarkable was, that although he was ever frowning with his eyes, his mouth was as continually grinning in a sort of laugh, such as you see in a man struck with a palsy in the head. He was the terror of all the children, and it was said the dogs never barked at him.

I found him in the hollow, hard by the beech-tree, and had scarce time to fling my implements among the bushes before he saw me. He was standing looking over towards the old church, where there was a funeral procession; for that morning the neighbours were burying a young man that had taken laudanum for love two days before, but had only expired the previous evening.

As soon as the German beheld me, he started like a guilty man, and made as if he would have run away; but suddenly changing his mind, he stepped towards me, and just as we met he stooped down and pulled a flower that struck his eye. Then rising up, he grinned at me, and nodding, said, "Gooten morrow, mine prudder; it ish gooten dag!"—though what he meant by "*gooten dag*" I know no more than the man in the moon, having never studied German. I did not at all like his appearance in this spot at such a time; but I reflected at last that he was only culling simples, and had paused near the beech-tree to look at the funeral, as would have been extremely natural in any man. But I liked the appearance of the funeral still less at such a particular time, and I thought there was something ominous in it.

But my mind was fixed upon the treasure I was soon to enjoy too firmly to be long drawn off by any such doleful spectacle; and accordingly, having waited impatiently until the attendants on the funeral had all stalked away, as well as the German doctor, I stole towards the beech-tree, and surveyed the ground at its roots. There were some stones lying among them, which I removed, as well as the long grass that waved over their tops; and looking closely, I thought I could see among some of the smaller roots of the tree, that were pleached together on the surface of the earth, a sort of arrangement very much in shape of a grave. This was a new proof to me that the treasure lay below, and I considered that my good angel had platted these roots together, in order to direct me in what spot to dig.

I could scarce avoid beginning on the instant; but, I remembered, that was not the hour. I therefore concealed my spade and mattock, and went home; when the first thing I did was to hunt me up a book that had the Lord's prayer in it (for I feared to trust to my memory alone), and write this out backwards with the greatest care; and I then spent the remainder of the day in committing the words to memory in that order; but I found it a difficult task.

As the evening drew nigh, I found myself growing into such a pitch of excitement, that, fearing I should betray the secret to Jim Jumble, who was constantly prying in upon me, I resolved to walk to the village, and there remain until the hour for seeking the treasure should draw nigh. I had another reason for this step; for my watch having gone, some month or two before Julius Cesar, to satisfy a hungry fellow to whom I owed money, I knew not how to be certain of the hour, unless by learning it of some one in the village; and to the village I accordingly went soon after sunset.

CHAPTER XII.

SHEPPARD LEE VISITS THE VILLAGE, MAKES A PATRIOTIC SPEECH, AND LEAVES THE FENCE.

Having arrived at the village, I proceeded to a tavern, which was the chief place of resort, especially after nightfall, for all the idlers and topers of the town, of whom there were great numbers, the village at that time being a place of but little business.

I found some ten or a dozen already assembled in the bar-room, drinking brandy, smoking, chewing, talking politics, and swearing. I had no sooner entered than some of them, who were discoursing loudly concerning the purity and economy of the government, and the honesty of those who supported it, appealed to me (my electioneering pilgrimage through the country having caused me to be looked upon as quite a knowing politician) to assist them in the argument they were holding.

Remembering the scurvy way in which I had been treated by the party, I felt strongly tempted to give them a piece of my mind on the other side of the question; but I thought of my buried treasure, and conceiving it unwise to begin the quarrel at that time, I made them no answer, but sat down in a corner, where I hoped to escape observation. Here I employed myself conning over the prayer backwards, until I was assured I was perfect in the exercise.

I then—still keeping aloof from the company—gave my mind up to a consideration of what I should do when I had transferred Captain Kid's hoards of gold from the coffin to my house.

The first thing I resolved to do was to pay my debts, which, how greatly soever they oppressed me, were not actually very fearful in amount; after which I was determined to rebuild my house, restore my fields to their original condition, and go to law with Mr. Aikin Jones, who I had no doubt had cheated me out of my property. It did not occur to me that, by such a step, I should get rid of my second fortune as expeditiously as I had the first; all that I thought on was the satisfaction of having my revenge on the villain, whom I should have punished in perhaps a more summary way, had it not been for my respect for the laws, and my being naturally a peaceable man. But I did not think long of Mr. Jones; the idea of the great wealth I was soon to possess filled my mind, and I gave myself up to the most transporting reveries.

From these I was roused by hearing some one near me pronounce the words "*Captain Kid's money*"—the idea that was uppermost in my own mind; and looking round in a kind of perturbation, I saw a knot of people surrounding Feuerteufel, the German doctor, one of whom was discoursing on the subject of the treasure in the Owl-roost, and avowing his belief that he—that is, the German doctor—was conjuring after it; an imputation that gained great credit with the company, there being no other way to account for his visit to our village, and his constant perambulations through the woods and marshes in the neighbourhood of the Owl-roost.

The German doctor, to my great relief, replied to this charge by expanding his jaws as if he would have swallowed the speaker, though he was guilty of nothing beyond a laugh, which was in depth and quality of tone as if an empty hogshead had indulged in the same diversion. His voice was indeed prodigiously deep and hollow, and even his laugh had something in it solemn and lugubrious. "Mine friends," said he, in very bad English, "I fos can do men' creat t'ings; put I can no find no Captain Kitt's money not at all. I toes neffer looks for coldt, except in places fare Gott puts it; t'at iss, in t'a coldt-mines!" With that, he laughed again, and looking upon the people about him with great contempt, he walked up stairs to his chamber—for he lodged in the inn.

Soon after this occurrence, and just when I had sunk again into a revery, a man stepped up to me, and saluted me in a way well suited to startle me.

"Sir," said he, "friend Kill-deer, before you scratch your head any more on this bench, answer me a question. What do you go for,—brandy-toddy or gin-sling?"

It was Squire Higginson, and he looked very good-humoured and waggish; but as I had dreamed of him so often, and always as being in his grave-clothes, I was rather petrified at his appearance, as if it were that of a spectre, rather than a mortal man. As for our quarrel in the meadow, it had slipped my mind altogether, until, having recovered my composure a little, it was recalled to my recollection by the associations arising out of his words.

But I remembered the circumstance at last, and being moreover offended by his present freedom, which was nothing less than sheer impertinence, I told him I desired to have nothing to say to him; on which he fell into a passion, and told me "I might go to the devil for a ragamuffin and a turncoat politician." But, mad as he was, he ended his speech by bursting into a laugh, and then, tapping his forehead as before, and nodding his head and winking, he left the bar-room to seek his chamber —for *he* put up at the tavern, as well as the German doctor.

These insults threw me into some ferment, and being irritated still farther by the remarks of the company, especially when some one asked what the squire meant by calling me a "turncoat politician," I allowed myself to be thrown into a passion; in the course of which I gave such of my old friends as were present to know that I had forsworn their party, and considered it to be composed of a pack of the corruptest scoundrels in the country.

This unexpected denunciation produced a great explosion; my old friends fell upon me tooth and nail, as the saying is, reviling me as a traitor and apostate. But, on the other hand, those of the opposition who happened to be present ranged themselves on my side, applauding my honesty, judgment, and spirit to such a degree, that I was more than ever convinced I had been on the wrong side. I met reproaches with contempt, and threats with defiance; opposed words to words, and assertions to assertions (for, in politics, we do not make use of arguments); and finding myself triumphantly victorious, I mounted into a chair, and made a speech that was received by my new friends with roars of applause. Intoxicated with these marks of approbation, I launched at once into a sea of declamation, in which I might have tossed about during the whole night, had I not by chance, while balking for a word, rolled my eyes upon the clock that stood opposite to me in the bar, and perceived that it wanted just a quarter of an hour to twelve o'clock. In a moment I forgot every thing but the treasure that awaited me in the Owl-roost; I stopped short in the middle of a sentence, took one more look at the clock, and then, leaping down from the chair, rushed from the tavern without saying a word, and, to the amazement of friend and foe, ran at full speed out of the village; and this gait I continued until I had reached the old Swedes' Church; for I had taken the footpath that led in that direction.

CHAPTER XIII.

WHAT BEFELL THE AUTHOR ON HIS WAY TO THE OWL-ROOST.

As it was now the full of the moon, there was of course light enough for my purpose; but the sky was dappled with clouds very dense and heavy, some of which crossing the moon every minute or two, there was a constant alternation of light and darkness, so that the trees and all other objects were constantly changing their appearance, now starting up in bold relief, white and silvery from the darkness, and now vanishing again into gloom.

A cloud passed over the moon just as I reached the old church; and the wall of the burial-ground having fallen down at a certain place, where the rubbish obstructed the path, it was my ill luck to break my shin against a fragment; the pain of which caused me to utter a loud groan. To my amazement and horror, this interjection of suffering was echoed from the grave-yard hard by, a voice screaming out in awful tones, "O Lord! O Lord!" and casting my eyes round, I beheld, as I thought, three or four shapes, that I deemed nothing less than devils incarnate, dancing about among the tomb-stones.

I was seized with such terror at this sight, that, forgetting my hurt and the treasure together, I took to my heels, and did not cease running until I had left the church some quarter of a mile behind me; and I am not certain I should have come to a halt then, had it not been my fate to tumble over a cow that lay ruminating on the path; whereby, besides half breaking my neck, and cruelly scratching my nose, I stunned myself to that degree, that it was some two or three minutes before I was able to rise.

I had thus time to recollect myself, and reflect that I was running away from Captain Kid's money, the idea of losing which was not to be tolerated a moment.

But how to get to the Owl-roost without falling into the hands of the devils or spectres at the old church, was what gave me infinite concern. The midnight hour—the only one for attempting the treasure with success— was now close at hand; so that there was no time left me to reach the place by a roundabout course through the woods to the right, or over the meadows to the left. I must pass the old church, or I must perhaps give up the treasure.

There was no time to deliberate; the figures I had seen, and the cries I had heard, might have been coinages of my own brain; nay, the latter were perhaps, after all, only the echoes of my own voice, distorted into something terrible by my fears. I was not naturally superstitious, and had never before believed in ghosts. But I cannot recollect what precise arguments occurred to me at that moment, to cause me to banish my fears. The hope of making my fortune was doubtless the strongest of all; and the moon suddenly shining out with the effulgence almost of day, I became greatly imboldened, and, in a word, set forward again, resolved, if met by a second apparition, and driven to flight, to fly, not backwards, but *forwards*,—that is, in the direction of the Owl-roost.

On this occasion, it was my fortune to be saluted by an owl that sat on the old wall among some bushes, and hooted at me as I went by; and notwithstanding that the sound was extremely familiar to my ears, I was thrown into a panic, and took to my heels as before; though, as I had resolved, I ran onward, pursuing the path to the swamp. It is quite possible there may have been a crew of imps and disimbodied spirits jumping among the graves as before; but, as I had the good fortune to be frightened before I caught sight of them, I did not stop to look for them; and, for the same reason, I heard no more awful voices shrieking in my ears. I reached the Owl-roost and the memorable beech-tree, where the necessity of acting with all speed helped me to get rid of my terror. I knew that I had not a moment to spare, and running to the bushes where I had hidden my mattock and spade, I fetched them to the tree, and instantly began to dig, not forgetting to pray backwards all the while, as hard as I could.

CHAPTER XIV.

SHEPPARD LEE DIGS FOR THE BURIED TREASURE, BUT MAKES A BLOW WITH THE MATTOCK IN THE WRONG PLACE.

I was but an ill hand at labour, and of the use of the spade and mattock I knew nothing. The nature of the ground in which I was digging made the task especially difficult and disagreeable. There were many big stones scattered about in the earth, which jarred my arms horribly whenever I stuck them; so that (all my efforts to the contrary notwithstanding) I was, every minute or two, interrupting my prayer with expressions which were neither wise nor religious, but highly expressive of my torture of body and mind. And then I was digging among the toughest and vilest roots in the world, some of which I thought I should never get through; for I had not remembered to provide myself with an axe, and I was afraid to go home for one, lest some evil accident or discovery might rob me of the expected treasure.

Accordingly, I had to do with a tougher piece of labour than I had ever undertaken before in my whole life; and I reckon I worked a full hour and a half, before I had got the hole I was excavating as deep as I supposed would be necessary. I succeeded at last, however, in throwing out so much earth, that when I measured the depth of the pit with my spade, I found the handle just on a level with the surface of the ground.

But I was not so near the treasure as I supposed; I struck my mattock into the clay, scarce doubting that I should hear the ring of the iron coffin. Instead of reaching that, however, I struck a great stone, and with a force that made the mattock-helve fly out of my hands to my chin, which it saluted with a vigour that set all my teeth to rattling, knocking me down into the bargain.

Having recovered from the effects of this blow, I fell to work again, thumping and delving until I had excavated to the depth of at least five feet. My heart began to fail me, as well as my strength, as I got so deep into the earth without finding the gold; for I began to fear lest my dreams had, after all, deceived me. In my agitation of mind, I handled my tools so blindly, that I succeeded in lodging my mattock, which was aimed furiously at a root, among the toes of my right foot; and the pain was so horribly acute, that I leaped howling out of the pit, and sinking down upon the grass, fell straightway into a trance.

CHAPTER XV.

IN WHICH SHEPPARD LEE FINDS HIMSELF IN A QUANDARY WHICH THE READER WILL ALLOW TO BE THE MOST WONDERFUL AND LAMENTABLE EVER KNOWN TO A HUMAN BEING.

When I awoke from this trance, it was almost daybreak.

I recovered in some confusion of mind, and did not for a moment notice that I was moving away from the place of my disaster; but I perceived there was something strange in my feelings and sensations. I felt exceedingly light and buoyant, as if a load had been taken, not merely from my mind, but from my body; it seemed to me as if I had the power of moving whither I would without exertion, and I fancied that I swept along without putting my feet to the ground. Nay, I had a notion that I was passing among shrubs and bushes, without experiencing from them any hinderance to my progress whatever. I felt no pain in my foot, which I had hit such a violent blow, and none in my hands, that had been wofully blistered by my work; nor had I the slightest feeling of weariness or fatigue. On the whole, my sensations were highly novel and agreeable; but before I had time to analyze them, or to wonder at the change, I remembered that I was wandering away from the buried treasure.

I returned to the spot, but only to be riveted to the earth in astonishment. I saw, stretched on the grass, just on the verge of the pit, the dead body of a man; but what was my horror, when, perusing the ashy features in the light of the moon, I perceived my own countenance! It was no illusion; it was *my* face, *my* figure, and dressed in *my* clothes; and the whole presented the appearance of perfect death.

The sight was as bewildering as it was shocking; and the whole state of things was not more terrifying than inexplicable. *There* I lay on the ground, stiff and lifeless; and *here* I stood on my feet, alive, and surveying my own corpse, stretched before me. But I forgot my extraordinary duality in my concern for myself—that is to say, for that part of me, that *eidolon*, or representative, or duplicate of me, that was stretched on the grass, I stooped down to raise the figure from the earth, in an instinctive desire to give myself aid, but in vain; I could not lift the body; it did not seem to me that I could even *touch it*,—my fingers, strive as I might, I could not bring into contact with it.

My condition, or *conditions* (for I was no longer of the singular number) at this time, can be understood only by comparing my confusion of senses and sensations to that which occurs in a dream, when one beholds himself dead, surveys his body, and philosophizes or laments, and is, all the time, to all intents and purposes, without being surprised at it, *two persons*, one of which lives and observes, while the other is wholly defunct. Thus I was, or appeared to be, without bestowing any reflection upon such an extraordinary circumstance, or being even conscious of it, two persons; in one of which I lived, but forgot my existence, while trembling at the death that had overcome me in the other. My true situation I did not yet comprehend, nor even dream of; though it soon turned out to be natural enough, and I understood it.

I was entirely overcome with horror at my unfortunate condition; and seeing that I was myself unable to render myself any assistance, I ran, upon an impulse of instinct, to the nearest quarter where it was to be obtained. This was at the cottage, or little farmhouse, which I spoke of before as standing on the by-road, a little beyond the old church. It was occupied by a man named Turnbuckle, whom I knew very well, and who was a very industrious, honest man, although a tenant of Mr. Aikin Jones.

I arrived at his house in an amazingly short space of time, rather flying, as it seemed to me, through the air, than running over the marsh and up the rugged hill. It was the gray of the morning, when I reached his house, and the family was just stirring within. As I ran towards the door, his dogs, of which he had a goodly number, as is common with poor men, set up a dismal howling, clapped their tails between their legs, and sneaked off among the bushes; a thing that surprised me much, for they were usually very savage of temper. I called to Turnbuckle by name, and that in a voice so piteous that, in half a minute, he and his eldest son came tumbling out of the house in the greatest haste and wonder. No sooner, however, had they cast eyes on me, than they uttered fearful cries; the old man fell flat on his face, as if in a fit, and the son ran back into the house, as if frightened out of his senses.

"Help me, Thomas Turnbuckle," said I; "I am lying dead under the beech-tree in the hollow: come along and give me help."

But the old man only answered by groaning and crying; and at that moment the door opened, and his eldest son appeared with a gun, which he fired at me, to my inexpressible terror.

But if I was frightened at this, how much more was I horrified when the old man, leaping up at the discharge, roared out, "O Lord! a ghost! a ghost!" and ran into the house.

I perceived it all in a moment: the howling of the dogs, which they still kept up from among the bushes,—the fear of Turnbuckle and his family, all of whom, old and young, male and female, were now squeaking in the house, as if Old Nick had got among them,—my being in two places together, and a thousand other circumstances that now occurred to me, apprized me of the dreadful fact, which I had not before suspected: I was a dead man!—my body lay in the marsh under the beech-tree, and it was my spirit that was wandering about in search of assistance!

As this terrible idea flashed across my mind, and I saw that I was a ghost, I was as much frightened as the Turnbuckles had been, and I took to my heels to fly from myself, until I recollected myself a little, and thought of the absurdity of such a proceeding. But even this fatal conception did not remove my anxiety in relation to my poor body,—or *myself*, as I could not help regarding my body; and I ran back to the beech-tree in a kind of distraction, hoping I might have been revived and resuscitated in my absence.

I reached the pit, and stared wildly about me—my body was gone,—vanished! I looked into the hole I had excavated; there was nothing in it but the spade and mattock, and my hat, which had fallen from my head when I leaped out of it, after hurting my foot. I stared round me again; the print of my body in the grass, where it had lain, was quite perceptible (for it was now almost broad day), but there was no body there, and no other vestige excepting one of my shoes, which was torn and bloody, being the identical one I had worn on the foot hurt by the mattock.

CHAPTER XVI.

SHEPPARD LEE FINDS COMFORT WHEN HE LEAST EXPECTS IT. THE EXTRAORDINARY CLOSE OF THE CATASTROPHE.

What had become of me? that is, what had become of my body? Its disappearance threw me into a phrensy; and I was about to run home, and summon old Jim Jumble to help me look for it, when I heard a dog yelping and whining in a peculiarly doleful manner, at some little distance down in the meadow; and I instantly ran in that direction, thinking that perhaps the bloodthirsty beast might be at that very moment dragging it away to devour it,—or hoping, at the least, to light upon some one who could give me an account of it.

I ran to a place in the edge of the marsh where were some willow-trees, and an old worm fence, the latter overgrown with briers and elder-bushes; and there, to my exceeding surprise, I discovered the body of Squire Higginson (for he was stone dead), lying against the fence, which was broken, his head down, and his heels resting against the rails, and looking as if, while climbing it, he had fallen down and broken his neck. His gun was lying at his side, undischarged, and his dog, whose yelping had brought me to the spot, was standing by; but I must add, that, as soon as I approached him, the animal betrayed as much terror as Turnbuckle's dogs had done, and ran howling away in the same manner.

Greatly incensed as I had been with Squire Higginson, I felt some concern to see him lying in this lamentable condition, his face blackened with blood, as if he had perished from suffocation; and stooping down, I endeavoured to take off his neckcloth and raise his head, in the hope that he might yet recover. But I reckoned without my host,—I had forgotten that I was a mere phantom or spirit, possessing no muscular power whatever, because no muscles; for, even in walking and running, as I was now aware, I was impelled by some unknown power within me, and not at all carried by my legs. I could not bring my hand into contact either with his cravat or head, and for a good reason, seeing there was no substance in me whatever, but all spirit.

I therefore ceased my endeavours, and began to moralize, in a mournful mood, upon his condition and mine. He was dead, and so was I; but there seemed to be this difference between us, namely, that I had lost my body, and he his soul,—for after looking hard about me, I could see nothing of it.

His body, as it lay there in the bushes, was perfectly useless to him, and to all the world beside; and my spirit, as was clear enough, was in a similar predicament. Why might I not, that is to say, my spirit,—deprived by an unhappy accident of its natural dwelling,—take possession of a tenement which there remained no spirit to claim, and thus, uniting interests together, as two feeble factions unite together in the political world, become a body possessing life, strength, and usefulness?

As soon as this idea entered my mind (or *me*, for I was all mind), I was seized with the envy that possessed me when I first met the squire shooting over my marshes. "How much better it would be," I thought, "to inhabit his body than my own! In my own fleshly casing, I should revive only to poverty and trouble;" (I had forgot all about Captain Kid's money) "whereas, if once in the body of Squire Higginson, I should step out into the world to possess riches, respect, content, and all that man covets. Oh that I might be Squire Higginson!" I cried.

The words were scarce out of my mouth, before I felt myself vanishing, as it were, into the dead man's nostrils, into which I—that is to say, my spirit—rushed like a breeze of air; and the very next moment I found myself kicking the fence to pieces in a lusty effort to rise to my feet, and feeling as if I had just tumbled over it.

"The devil take the fence, and that Jersey kill-deer that keeps it in such bad order!" I cried, as I rose up, snatching at my gun, and whistling for my dog Ponto. *My* dog Ponto! It was even the truth; I was no more Sheppard Lee, the poor and discontented,—no longer a disimbodied spirit, wandering about only to frighten dogs out of their senses; but John Hazlewood Higginson, Esq., solid and substantial in purse and flesh, with a rosy face, and a heart as cheerful as the morning, which was now reddening over the whole east. If I had wanted any proof of the transformation beyond that furnished by my own senses and sensations, it would have been provided by my dog Ponto, who now came running up, leaping on and about me with the most extravagant joy.

"God be thanked!" I cried, dancing about as joyously as the dog; "I am now a respectable man, with my pockets full of money. Farewell, then, you poor miserable Sheppard Lee! you ragamuffin! you poor wretched shote! you half-starved old sand-field Jersey kill-deer! you vagabond! you beggar! you Dicky Dout, with the wrong place in your upper story! you are now a gentleman and a man of substance, and a happy dog into the bargain.

Ha, ha, ha!" and here I fell a laughing out of pure joy; and giving my dog Ponto a buss, as if that were the most natural act in the world, and a customary way of showing my satisfaction, I began to stalk towards my old ruined house, without exactly knowing for what purpose, but having some vague idea about me, that I would set old Jim Jumble and his wife Dinah to shouting and dancing; an amusement I would willingly have seen the whole world engaged in at that moment.

CHAPTER XVII.

A NATURAL MISTAKE, WHICH, ALTHOUGH IT PROCURES THE AUTHOR A ROUGH RECEPTION AT HIS OWN HOUSE, HAS YET THE GOOD EFFECT TO TEACH HIM THE PROPRIETY OF ADAPTING HIS MANNERS TO HIS CONDITION.

I had not walked twenty yards, before a woodcock that was feeding on the edge of the marsh started up from under my nose, when, clapping my gun to my shoulder, I let fly at him, and down he came.

"Aha, Ponto!" said I, "when did I ever fail to bring down a woodcock? Bring it along, Ponto, you rascal.—Rum-te, ti, ti! rum-te, ti, ti!" and I went on my way singing for pure joy, without pausing to recharge, or to bag my game. I reached my old house, and began to roar out, without reflecting that I was now something more than Sheppard Lee, "Hillo! Jim Jumble, you old rascal! get up and let me in."

"What you want, hah?" said old Jim, poking his head from the garret-window of the kitchen, and looking as sour as a persimmon before frost. "Guess Massa Squire Higginson drunk, hah? What you want? S'pose I'm gwyin to git up afo' sunrise for not'in', and for anybody but my Massa Sheppard?"

"Why, you old dog," said I, in a passion, "I am your master Sheppard; that is, your master John Hazlewood Higginson, Esquire; for as for Sheppard Lee, the Jersey kill-deer, I've finished him, you rascal; you'll never see him more. So get down, and let me into the house, or I'll—"

"You will, hah?" said Jim; "you will *what?*"

"I'll shoot you, you insolent scoundrel!" I exclaimed, in a rage,—as if it were the most natural thing in the world for me to be in one; and as I spoke, I raised my piece; when "Bow—wow—wough!" went my old dog Bull, who had not bitten a man for two years, but who now rushed from his kennel under the porch, and seized me by the leg.

"Get out, Bull, you rascal!" said I, but he only bit the harder; which threw me into such a fury that I clapped the muzzle of my gun to his side, and, having one charge remaining, blew him to pieces.

"Golla-matty!" said old Jim, from the window, whence he had surveyed the combat; "golla-matty! shoot old Bull!"

And with that the black villain snatched up the half of a brick, which I suppose he kept to daunt unwelcome visiters, and taking aim at me, he cast it so well as to bring it right against my left ear, and so tumbled me to the ground. I would have blown the rascal's brains out, in requital of this assault, had there been a charge left in my piece, or had he given me time to reload; but as soon as he had cast the brick, he ran from the window, and then reappeared, holding out an old musket that, I remembered, he kept to shoot wild ducks and muskrats in the neighbouring marsh with. Seeing this formidable weapon, and not knowing but that the desperado would fire upon me, I was forced to beat a retreat, which I did in double quick time, being soon joined by my dog Ponto, who had fled, like a coward, at the first bow-wough of the bulldog, and saluted in my flight by the amiable tones of Dinah, who now thrust her head from the window, beside Jim's, and abused me as long as I could hear.

BOOK II.
CONTAINING SUNDRY ILLUSTRATIONS OF THE ADVANTAGES OF GOOD LIVING, WITH A FEW CHAPTERS ON DOMESTIC FELICITY.

CHAPTER I.

SOME PASSAGES IN THE LIFE OF JOHN H. HIGGINSON, ESQ., THE HAPPY SPORTSMAN; WITH A SURPRISING AFFLICTION THAT BEFELL THE AUTHOR.

I went off in a towering rage, to think of the reception I had met, and that too after an absence of a whole night. I had been bitten by my own dog, and driven from my own doors by my own servants! But there was something in these circumstances to admonish me of the change that had come over me. They reminded me of a fact that was not always present to my thoughts,—to wit, that I was no longer Sheppard Lee, but Mr. John Hazlewood Higginson, a very different sort of personage altogether.

To account for my forgetfulness of this important transformation, I must relate that, although I had acquired along with his body all the peculiarities of feeling, propensity, conversation, and conduct of Squire Higginson, I had not entirely lost those that belonged to Sheppard Lee. In fact, I may be said to have possessed, at that time, two different characters, one of which now governed me, and now the other; though the squire's, it must be confessed, was greatly predominant. Thus, the moment after the transformation, I found myself endowed with a passion for shooting, as if I had had it all my life long, a buoyant tone of mind, and, in addition, as I by-and-by discovered, with somewhat a hot temper; none of which had ever been known to me before. The difficulty was, that I could not immediately shake off my old Sheppard Lee habits; and the influence of these, perhaps (if one must scrutinize into the matter), more than the absolute retention of any other native peculiarities, drove me into the inconsistencies of which I was for a short time guilty. But I will not trouble the reader with philosophizing.

I perceived, from the repulse I had received from Jim Jumble, that it now became me to sink his old master altogether, which I was very well content to do, and resolved accordingly; although I could not help thinking, as I strode over the forty-acre farm, how much satisfaction I should have, now that I was a rich man, in putting it into fine order. But these thoughts were soon driven from my mind by Ponto making a set at some game, and in a moment I was banging away, right and left, and slaughtering the birds in the finest style imaginable.

Oh, the delights of shooting woodcock! It is rather hot work, though, of a midsummer day; and notwithstanding the prodigious satisfaction I had in pursuing the sport, I felt that my satisfaction would have been still greater, had I been a few stone lighter. I began to think Squire Higginson's fat rather inconvenient; and I had the same opinion of a touch of asthma, or something of that nature, which I found in his lungs; and, besides, there was a sort of whizzing, and humming, and spinning in my head, where they had been all the morning which were not altogether agreeable.

In consequence of these infirmities of my new body, I began, after a while, to weary of the sport; and was just on the point of setting off to the village to get my dinner, when a crowd of men made their appearance in the marsh, and setting up a great shout at sight of me, began to run towards me. I could not conceive the cause of such a concourse, nor could I imagine for what reason they directed their steps towards me; but hearing them utter the most furious cries, and perceiving that a multitude of dogs they had with them were rushing against me, as if to devour me, I was seized with alarm, and began to retreat towards a wood that was not far off.

This evidence of terror on my part only caused the people to utter louder and more savage cries, besides setting the dogs to running faster; and these ferocious animals gaining upon me, and being on the point of tearing me to pieces, I was obliged to let fly my piece among them, whereby I shot one dead, and disabled two or three others. I then defended myself with the breech of my gun, until the men came up; one of whom tripped up my heels, while the others seized and disarmed me, crying out "that I was a murderer; that I was found out, and should be hanged, if there was any law in the county."

I was confounded at this charge; but how much greater was my amazement, when I understood, as they haled me along towards the village, which they did very roughly, that I was accused of having murdered Sheppard Lee—that is, my own identical self!

This accusation appeared to me so preposterous, that in spite of my indignation (for my fears had now subsided), I burst into a laugh; which only made them rail at me more furiously than I can express. "Hear him!" said they; "he laughs! He thinks, because he is a rich man, he can shoot any poor man he pleases, and buy himself off. But we will show him there's law in Jersey for aristocrats as well as poor men, and that we can hang a purse-proud man as soon as a beggar."

And so they went on reviling me as if I had been the greatest criminal in the land, and dragging me, as they said, to a squire, who would soon show me what law was.

CHAPTER II.

THE AUTHOR, BEING IN PRISON, MAKES A CONFIDANT OF A DEPUTY ATTORNEY-GENERAL.— THE INCONVENIENCE OF TELLING A TRUTH WHICH HAPPENS TO BE SOMEWHAT INCREDIBLE.

My wrath gave way when I found myself in prison; and hearing from the jailer that the grand jury was then in session, and the prosecuting attorney actually engaged in framing a bill of endictment against me, to send up to its members, I began to think the matter rather serious, and resolved to end it before it proceeded further.

I had already experienced the ill effects of attempting to sustain the character of Sheppard Lee while in the body of another man, and for this reason was resolved to be more cautious for the future; but I now perceived I had no better way of relieving myself of my troubles than by making the prosecutor, who had been an old friend of mine, and had always treated me with respect, acquainted with my transformation; after which, I had no doubt, he would throw his bill of endictment into the fire. I sent for him accordingly; but was obliged to repeat the message before he thought fit to make his appearance.

"You have perhaps made a mistake, Mr. Higginson," said he, as he entered. "You have occasion for counsel, but none that I can imagine for *me*; for as to my giving you any advice in this unfortunate affair—".

"The devil take the affair," said I, in no amiable voice; "it was to get rid of it entirely that I sent for you; for I must stop that cursed endictment of yours. I don't want it said of me hereafter that I was once in my life endicted for a felony."

"Oh, sir," said he, with a smile, "we are in no hurry about these things; the bill will lie over till we can procure a little more evidence, and some of a better quality. Don't be in any alarm; but allow me to recommend you to employ counsel. My friend Sharphead, I think, will be your best man."

"I don't want any counsel," said I, "and Sharphead may go to the devil; I want to confide to you the true secret of this extraordinary affair."

"Faith, sir," said he, looking at me in surprise, "if you can do that, the case is not so ridiculous as I thought. Really, Mr. Higginson, I was rather amused than otherwise at the charge brought against you, not supposing you knew any thing of, or had any connexion whatever with, the disappearance of poor Sheppard Lee. But, since you talk of secrets, sir, I must inform you, I am not the person you should make any confessions to. I must again recommend you to employ counsel."

And with that he was about leaving me, but I arrested him. "Stop, Jack," said I (his name was John Darling, and he is very well known in the state, though he was turned out of office), "you and I are old friends, and we must have a talk together."

At these words he gave me a hard stare, looking more astonished than ever.

"Jack," said I, taking him by the hand, "I'll make you stare harder than that. Sheppard Lee is no more dead than I am; though, as for his body, I believe Old Nick has got it. Now, my boy, I take it you will act as a friend in this matter, and not blab my secret: but the truth is, it is John H. Higginson who is dead, and *I* who am living."

"The deuse it is!" said the lawyer, whose amazement set me into a capital humour. "And pray, sir," he added, "if John H. Higginson is dead, who are *you?*"

"Sheppard Lee!" said I, bursting into a laugh, "only that you see me now in John H. Higginson's body."

I then proceeded to inform him, as I have informed the reader, of my digging for the treasure, of my sudden death, of the visit of my spirit to old Turnbuckle's, of the disappearance of my body, of my finding and entering that of Squire Higginson, in which he now saw me, and, in fine, of all the other circumstances connected with the transformation; all which he heard like a man whom the novelty of the relation astounded into marble.

"Upon my soul," said he, when I had done, "you have told me a most surprising story. And so you really think yourself Sheppard Lee—that is, Sheppard Lee's spirit in Squire Higginson's body?"

"*Think* myself, sir!" said I, a little fiercely.

"Do you presume to slight my veracity, sir? or to doubt my common sense?"

"By no means," said he; "I have the utmost respect for both. Your story has completely satisfied me of your innocence. A most wonderful story, sir! truly, a most wonderful story!" And repeating these words over and over again, he fell to nodding his head and musing, staring at me all the time, like one who is lost in wonder; and then suddenly rousing up, he burst into a roar of laughter. Seeing that I was incensed at his merriment, he hastened to apologize, declaring that he was not laughing at my story, but at the absurdity he had been so nigh committing in endicting me for my own murder; and he added, that my relation was altogether the most remarkable he had ever heard in his life.

I then gave him to understand, I expected, for very good and obvious reasons, that he would keep the story to himself; which he faithfully promised. He then fell to cross-questioning me in relation to different points; and he was particularly curious to know what I supposed had become of my body; when, not being able to satisfy him on that point, he himself suggested that perhaps Squire Higginson's spirit had taken possession of it, as I had done with his, and carried it off for some purpose or other, and that we should soon have news of him; an idea that was so agreeable to him, that he fell to laughing as hard as ever. "Sir," said he, shaking me by the hand in excellent good-humour, "we will soon have you out of this dog-hole, and that without betraying your secret. Heaven forbid I should spoil the good fortune of my old friend Sheppard Lee! No, sir, I am no tale-bearer, or blabber of secrets. Comfort yourself, sir; I never had the least idea of endicting you on this absurd charge. Nobody believes Sheppard Lee has been murdered by you, nor, indeed, by any one else. No, poor devil! the general opinion now is, that he has taken himself off, to get clear of duns and sheriffs; and as for the bloody shoe and hat, why that's a common way of turning pursuers off the scent, by throwing dust in their eyes. The charge will be abandoned, sir; you will be liberated, and may, if you like such amusement, prosecute your captors by the dozen for assault and battery. Farewell, Mr. Higginson,—that is, Mr. Lee; fortune smiles upon you at last; and you are a happy,—a wonderful man, sir.—Farewell!"

The attorney then left me; and so much diverted was he by my adventure, that I could hear him indulge peal after peal of mirth, until he had got out of the prison.

Now it may be supposed that my story, from its reasonableness, carried conviction to the attorney's mind; and so I was persuaded. But I reckoned without my host; the hypocritical gentleman did not believe a word of it, however much he pretended to do so. But in this he was like the rest of the fraternity: I never, indeed, knew a lawyer to believe any thing unless he was paid for it; and I forgot to present my gentleman a fee. My story, therefore, not being paid for, or proved according to law, only convinced this skeptical person that I—"the unfortunate Higginson," as he called me— had suddenly lost my senses, and gone staring mad; and in consequence, disregarding all his promises of secrecy, he ran over the whole village, diverting every one he could lay hands on with an account of "the poor squire's hallucination," as he termed it—that is to say, his conceit that his body was now inhabited by the soul of Sheppard Lee.

But to give a certain personage his due, or one of that personage's representatives, I must confess that Darling, who was at bottom a good-natured fellow, recollected one part of his promise, and took measures to effect my discharge from prison; which was no very difficult matter, people being now pretty well aware of the folly of the charge they had brought against me, and the absurdity of the evidence designed to support it. The opinion was already entertained that poor Sheppard Lee, instead of being murdered, had taken himself out of the neighbourhood to avoid his creditors, having left his hat and shoe in the swamp only as blinds to those who might be most anxious to secure his person; and pursuers had already left the village to discover his place of concealment.

CHAPTER III.

SHEPPARD LEE IS VISITED BY NEW FRIENDS, RELEASED FROM PRISON, AND CARRIED TO HIS NEW PLACE OF ABODE.

Another service that the attorney did me, according to the jailer, through whom I discovered all these things, was to despatch a messenger to my friends in Philadelphia, with the news of my insanity and imprisonment, and a request that they should send proper persons to take charge of me after being liberated: and I was roused the following morning by the appearance of some half a dozen kinsmen who had come to the village for that purpose, fully persuaded that they should find me a raging lunatic.

But the jailer's information had set me to reflecting upon my difficulties, all of which, as I clearly perceived, were owing to my indiscretion in attempting to keep up the character of Sheppard Lee while in another man's body. I saw the necessity I was now placed under to be Mr. John H. Higginson, and nobody else, for the future; and so I resolved to be—for I did not like the idea of being clapped into a mad-house by my new friends.

Yet they took me so much by surprise that I was guilty of some few inconsistencies; for it was not immediately that I felt myself at case in my new character.

The truth is, my situation was peculiar and embarrassing. With the body of Mr. Higginson, I had acquired all his distinctive peculiarities, as I mentioned before. But many of these were in a manner stupified within me, and required to be renewed, or resuscitated, by processes of association. I was like a man who has been roused from a lethargy, which had destroyed or obscured his memory, though not his instincts; and who betrays complete ignorance of past events, and forgetfulness of old friends, until some accidental circumstance—a casual reference to some past event, the tone of a voice, or other such cause—recalls him, it may be, to sudden and complete, though usually imperfect, consciousness.

Thus, when I was roused up in the morning, and beheld a good-looking personage of about my own years shaking me by the shoulder, I regarded him only as some impertinent stranger intruding upon my privacy, saluted him with divers epithets expressive of rage and indignation, and concluded by asking him "who the devil he was?"

"What! *I?*" said he, with the most doleful visage in the world; "why, Timothy—that is, Tim Doolittle, your brother-in-law—Don't you know me?"

And "Don't you know *me?* and *me?* and *me?* your cousin, Tom This, and your old friend, Dick That?" cried they all, with horrible long faces; the oddity of which after a while set me a laughing, especially when I came to recollect them all, as I did by-and-by when they had pronounced their names; for at each name it seemed to me as if a film fell from my eyes, and some spirit within awakened me to a vague recollection of the person to whom it belonged. In a word, I became aware that I was surrounded by a knot of my oldest and best friends, all of them excellent jolly dogs and good fellows, who were come to escort me home, and assured me that I was no longer a prisoner.

I shook them all by the hand, and contrasting for a moment in my mind the melancholy condition in which I had lived as Sheppard Lee, with my present glorious state, surrounded by friends, and conscious of possessing lands, houses, stocks, Schuylkill coal-mines, and the Lord knows what other goods beside, I fell into a rapture, danced about my cell, and hugged every person present, as well as the jailer, and my old friend Darling, the attorney, who happened at that moment to enter.

"Bravo!" said Tim Doolittle; "now you're the true Jack Higginson again; and I don't believe you are mad a bit."

"Mad!" said I, thinking it needful to explain away that imputation, "No, and I never was. I tumbled over an old rotten fence, and hurt my head, which was, in consequence, in a whiz all day yesterday; but now it is clear enough. I think I said some silly things about one thing and another; but that's neither here nor there."

"Ah!" said Tim Doolittle, touching his forehead and looking as grave as a bullfrog, "it's well it's no worse; for I always thought you had a turn for apoplexy. But I'm glad you are so well; it will be good news for poor Margaret."

"Margaret! who the deuse is she?" said I, feeling quite strange at the name.

"Why, my poor sister, your wife, to be sure," said he.

My *wife!!!* I recollected that I *had* a wife; but the recollection made me feel, I knew not exactly why, as if I had been suddenly soused into cold water. It was a highly uncomfortable idea, and accordingly I hastened to get rid of it.

"Let us leave this confounded place," I said; and we left the prison.

The prospect of a fine sunshiny day infused animation into my mind, which was vastly increased when I stepped into a splendid new barouche, with a pair of bay horses worth a thousand dollars—for so much Tim gave me to understand *I*—that is to say, my prototype—had given for them scarce a month before—the whole establishment being therefore my own! "What a happy man am I! Ah! poor miserable Sheppard Lee! Farewell now to poverty! farewell to discontent!"

Such were my secret ejaculations as we set out in my splendid barouche, followed by a train of gigs and carriages that contained my friends. I esteemed myself the happiest man in the world; and I gave my last sigh to the memory of Sheppard Lee.

What a glorious time we had of it on our way to Philadelphia! I found myself the richest man in the company—my pocketbook was full of bank-notes—and I resolved to give my friends a blow-out. We stopped at a certain village, and at a certain hotel therein, the master of which prepares the best dinners, and has the best butt of genuine Madeira, in all New-Jersey. "Let us rest and rejoice," I said, "and we will drive into town after nightfall."

My friends agreed; we ate, drank, and were merry; and it was not until after sunrise the next morning that we found ourselves in Philadelphia, and in my—yes, excellent reader—in *my* house in Chestnut-street, south side, two doors from the corner of—But it is needless to be particular. The house is yet standing, in a highly aristocratic neighbourhood, and is not yet converted into a dry-goods shop.

I reached my house: I—But before I relate what befell me in that splendid pile of red bricks, which, like its neighbours, seems to be blushing all the year round at its naked simplicity, I must say a few words more of Sheppard Lee.

CHAPTER IV.

CONTAINING ILLUSTRATIONS OF THE ADVANTAGES OF DYING AN UNUSUAL DEATH, IN TIMES OF HIGH POLITICAL EXCITEMENT.

I never felt the slightest inclination to revisit the scenes of my late trouble and discontent; but the newspapers, which are the lights of the age, though occasionally somewhat smoky, acquainted me with the events that followed after my marvellous disappearance. "What has become of Sheppard Lee?" was the cry, after his creditors had sought for him in vain during a space of two weeks and more. No vestige of him was discovered, not the slightest clew to indicate his fate, beyond those already brought to light in the Owl-roost. It was impossible he could have fled without leaving some traces; and none were found. "And *why* should he fly?" men at last began to ask. He was in debt, it was true; but what could he gain by absconding, since his little property was necessarily left behind him?

In a word, the improbabilities of his having voluntarily fled were so great, that men began to recur to their original idea of his having been murdered. But why was he murdered? and by whom? Some few began to revive the charges against me—that is to say, against John H. Higginson; but brighter ideas were struck out, and John H. Higginson was forgotten. An old friend of mine, who never cared a fig for me, but who was ambitious to create a tumult, and become the leader of a party, got up in a public place, and recounted the history of William Morgan, and his mysterious abduction and murder by the masons of the empire state. A terrible agitation at once seized his listeners. "Poor, dear, unfortunate Sheppard Lee!" they cried; "the masons have Morganized him, for apostatizing from his oaths, and revealing the secrets of the society! Yes, he has been Morganized!" And, giving way to their rage, they were on the point of tarring and feathering all the free-masons they could lay their hands on; when, *presto*—as the conjurers say, they suddenly made discovery that the masons could not have murdered me for divulging secrets, inasmuch as I had never known them, nor for apostatizing, as I had never been a mason in my life.

But the tumult was not allowed to subside. My old friends of the administration, finding that their strength was dwindling away in the country, and dreading the event of the coming election, unless a reaction could be got up in their favour, suddenly burst into a fury, swore that I had been made away with by the opposition, on account of my remarkable zeal, energy, and success, as an electioneerer and political missionary; and taking my old hat and shoe, and carrying them round the village in solemn procession, they stopped in the market-place, where one of their chief orators—my faithful friend, the new postmaster—delivered a sort of funeral address, in which he compared the opponents of the administration to cut-throats and cannibals, pronounced them the enemies of liberty, swore that no honest patriot was safe among them, and declared—his declaration being illustrated by shouts, and groans, and grim faces—"that I had perished, the victim of a murderous opposition!"

But, as if that was not immortality enough for one of my humble pretensions, the opposition instantly turned the tables upon their accusers. Witnesses stepped forward to prove that, on the night when I was seen for the last time, I had, in the bar-room of the first hotel in the village, publicly denounced the hurrah party, as being based upon deception and fraud, and avowed my determination not only instantly to leave it, but to go my death thenceforth in opposition. "See the bloody vindictiveness and malice of the hurrah party!" they cried; "before the sun rose upon this unfortunate and honest man—honest, because he deserted his party the moment his eyes were opened to its corruption—he was a living man no longer. The bravoes of this horrible gang of mid-night murderers, who have trampled on our rights and liberties, and now trample on our lives, met the unlucky patriot as he returned to his lowly cot, and—just Heavens!—where was he now, save in his bloody and untimely grave? he, the humble, the unoffending, the honest, the universally-esteemed, the widely-beloved, the patriotic Sheppard Lee!—waylaid and ambushed! killed, slain, murdered, massacred! the victim of a despotic and vindictive cabal,—the martyr of liberty, the—"
In short, the noblest, honestest, dearest, best, and most ill-used creature that ever dabbled in the puddle of politics. One might suppose that this outcry of the antis, backed as it was by the full proof of my change of politics, would have stopped the mouths of the hurrah-boys. But it did no such thing; they only raved the louder. As for the proof of my backsliding, they treated that with contempt; proofs being as little regarded in politics as arguments. They accused the antis more zealously than before; and the antis recriminated with equal enthusiasm.

There were some men in the village who strove to appease the ferment, by directing suspicion upon the German doctor, and divers other personages, just as the humour of suspicion seized them, furiously accusing these suspected individuals of having had some hand in the catastrophe. But the German doctor and the other persons accused had nothing to do with politics, and were therefore suffered to go their ways. It is a great protection to one's reputation to keep clear of politics. The guilt of my murder was left to be borne by the hurrah-boys and the antis, one party or the other; but as the evidence was equally strong against either party, and just as strong against any one individual of either party as another, it resulted that I was murdered not only by both parties, but by every man of both parties;—a peculiarity in my history that proved me to have possessed, though I never dreamed it before, a vaster number both of energetic friends and bloodthirsty enemies (each man being both friend and enemy) than any other man in the whole world.

How the antis and the hurrah-boys settled the affair among them, I did not care to inquire. I was engrossed by the novelties and charms of a new being, and willing to forget that such a poor devil as Sheppard Lee had ever existed.

CHAPTER V.

THE TRUE MEANING OF THE WORD PODAGRA.

Let the reader judge of my transport, when my elegant new barouche and splendid pair of horses, that cost me a thousand dollars, drew up before my house in Chestnut-street. I stood upon the kerb-stone and surveyed it from top to bottom. The marble of the steps, basement, and window-sills was white as snow, and the bricks were redder than roses. The windows were of plate glass, and within them were curtains of crimson damask, fronted with hangings of white lace, as fine and lovely as a bride's veil of true Paris blonde; and a great bouquet of dahlias, wreathed around a blooming rose, glittered in each. It was evidently the house of a man of wealth and figure.

The neighbourhood, it was equally manifest, was of the highest vogue and distinction: on one side was the dwelling of a fashionable tailor, who built a house out of every ten coats that he cut; on the other side was the residence of a retired tavern-keeper; and right opposite, on the other side of the street, was the mansion of one of the first aristocrats in the town, who had had neither a tailor nor a tavern-keeper in the family for a space of three full generations. There was no end to the genteel people in my neighbourhood; here was the house of a firstrate lawyer, there of a shop-keeper who had not sold any thing by retail for ten years; here a Croesus of a carpenter who turned up his nose at the aristocrat, and there a Plutus of a note-shaver who looked with contempt on the gentleman of chips. In short, my house was in a highly fashionable neighbourhood; and I felt, as I mounted my marble steps, that Jack Higginson, the brewer (as my brother Tim always called me), was as genteel a fellow among them as you would find of a summer's day.

I entered the house as proud as Lucifer, telling my friends that they should crack a bottle or two of my best port; for Tim had given me a hint that my cellar contained some of the best in the world. "And," said Tim, giving me a wink, "we may take our fun now, as sister Margaret—" at that name I felt a cold creeping in my bones—"as sister Margaret is still in the country." The ague left me—"I did not think it," he continued, "worth while to alarm her."

"The Lord be thanked!" said I; though *why* I said it, I knew no more than the man in the moon.

We sat down, we drank, and we made merry—that is to say, *they* made merry: as for myself, a circumstance occurred which nipped my pleasure in the bud, and began to make me doubt whether, in exchanging the condition of Sheppard Lee for that of John H. Higginson, I had not made somewhat of a bad bargain.

I had managed, somehow or other, in the course of the night, to stump my toe, or wrench my foot; and, though the accident caused me but little inconvenience at the time, the member had begun gradually to feel uneasy; and now, as I sat at my table, it grew so painful that I was forced to draw off my boot. But this giving me little relief, and finding that my foot was swollen out of all shape and beauty, my brother Tim pronounced it a severe strain, and recommended that I should call in my family physician, Dr. Boneset, a very illustrious man, and fine fellow, who at that moment chanced to drive by in his coal-black gig, which looked, as physicians' gigs usually look, as if in mourning for a thousand departed patients.

"What's the matter?" said the doctor.

"Why, doctor," said I, "I have given my foot a confounded wrench; I scarce know how; but it is as big and as hot as a plum-pudding."

"Hum, ay!—very unlucky," said the doctor: "off with your stocking, and let me look at your tongue. Pulse quite feverish. Fine port!" he said, drinking off a glass that Tim had poured him, and cocking his eye like one who means to be witty, "fine port, sir; but one can't float in it for ever without paying port-charges. A very gentlemanly disease, at all events. It lies between port and porter."

"Port and porter! disease!" said I, slipping off my stocking as he directed, without well knowing what he meant. My foot was as red as a salamander, swelled beyond all expression, and, while I drew the stocking, it hurt me most horribly.

"Zounds doctor!" said I, "can that be a wrench?"

"No," said the doctor, "it's the wrencher—genuine *podagra*, 'pon honour."

"Podagra!" said I; "Podagra!" said Tim; and "Podagra!" said the others. "What's that?"

"Gout!" said the doctor.

"Gout!" cried my friends; "Gout!!" roared my brother Tim; and "Gout!!!" yelled I, starting from the doctor as if from an imp of darkness who had just come to make claim to me. It was the unluckiest leap in the world; I kicked over a chair as I started, and the touch was as if I had clapped my foot into the jaws of a roaring lion. Crunch went every bone; crack went every sinew; and such a yell as I set up was never before heard in Chestnut-street.

"You see, gentlemen—(I'll take another glass of that port, Mr. Doolittle)—you see what we must all come to! This is one of the small penalties one must pay for being a gentleman; when one dances, one must pay the piper. Now would my friend Higginson there give a whole year of his best brewing, that all the pale ale and purple port that have passed his lips had been nothing better than elder-wine and bonny-clabber. But never mind, my dear sir," said the son of Æsculapius, with a coolness that shocked me; "as long as it's only in your foot, it's a small matter."

"A small matter!"—I grinned at him; but the unfeeling wretch only repeated his words—"A small matter!"

I had never been sick before in my life. As John H. Higginson, my worst complaints had been only an occasional surfeit, or a moderate attack of booziness; and as Sheppard Lee, I had never known any disease except laziness, which, being chronic, I had grown so accustomed to that it never troubled me. But now, ah, *now*! my first step into the world of enjoyment was to be made on red-hot ploughshares and pokers; my first hour of a life of content was to be passed in grinning, and groaning, and—but it is hardly worth while to say it. The gout should be confined to religious people; for men of the world *will* swear, and that roundly.

For six days——six mortal days——did I lay upon my back, enduring such horrible twitches and twinges in my foot, that I was more than once on the point of ordering the doctor to cut it off; and I do not know how far that conceit might have gone, had not the heartless fellow, who, I believe, was all the while making game of my torments, assured me that the only effect of the dismemberment would be to drive the enemy into the other foot, where it would play the same tricks over again. "The gout," said he, "has as great an affection for the human body as a cat has for a house in which she has been well treated. When it once effects a lodgment, and feels itself comfortable—"

"Comfortable!" said I, with a groan.

"In good easy quarters—"

"Don't talk to me of *easy* quarters," said I; "for if I were hacked into quarters, and that by the clumsiest butcher in the town, I could not be more uneasy in every quarter."

"I am talking," said Dr. Boneset, "not of you, but of the disease; and what I meant to say was, that when it once finds itself at home, in a good wholesome corporation of a man, there you may expect to find it a tenant for life."

"For life!" said I. "I am the most wretched man in existence. Oh, Sheppard Lee! Sheppard Lee! what a fool were you to think yourself miserable!— Doctor, I shall go mad!"

"Not while you have the gout," said he; "'tis a sovereign protection against all that.—But let us look at your foot." And the awkward or malicious creature managed to drop a tortoise and gold snuff-box, of about a pound and a half weight, which he was always sporting, right upon the point of my great toe, while he was looking at it. Had it been a ton and a half instead of a pound and a half in weight, it could not have thrown me into greater torture; and the—the man!—he thought he had settled the matter by making me a handsome apology! He left me to endure my pangs, and to curse Squire Higginson's father, grandfather, great-grandfather, and, in general, all his forefathers, who had entailed such susceptible great toes upon the family. In a word, I was in such a horrible quandary, that I wished the devil would fly off with my new body, as he had done before with the old.

CHAPTER VI.

SHEPPARD LEE'S INTRODUCTION TO HIS WIFE, AND HIS SUSPICION THAT ALL IS NOT GOLD THAT GLISTENS.

But there is, as philosophers say, an unguent for every wound, a solace for every care; and it was my fate to experience the consolation that one provides beforehand against the gout, as well as all other ills man may anticipate, in the person of a faithful spouse. On the fourth day of my malady, and just at a moment when I was fairly yelling with pain, a lady, neither young nor beautiful, but dressed like a princess, save that her shoes were down at heel, and her bonnet somewhat awry, stepped up to my bedside, seized me by the hand, and crying out, "Oh my poor dear husband!" burst into tears.

Her appearance acted like a charm; even my foot, that seemed to be roasting over one of Nott's patent anthracite blazers, grew cool and comfortable in the chill that was diffused over my whole body. Complaint was silent at the sight of her; pain vanished at her touch; I forgot that I had the gout, and remembered only that I had a wife.

I was struck dumb, and presume I should not have groaned again for twenty-four hours, had not my consort, in the exuberance of her affection and grief, thrown her arms around my neck, and thereby brought the whole weight of her body upon my foot, which, after having tried all parts of the bed, I had at last lodged upon the very extremity of the feathers; by which act of endearment my poor unfortunate limb was crushed against the horrible log of mahogany that made one side of the bed-stead, and ground to pieces. Had my wife been my wife twenty times over, I must have uttered just as loud a cry as I did, and repeated it just as often.

She started up, and regarded me with severity.

"Is that the way you use me?" said she.—I believe I had rather pushed her away; but *how* could I help it?—"Is that the way you welcome me home, whither I have come,—leaving kinsfolk and friends,—to nurse you? Barbarous man, you hate me! yes, and besides having no longer any love for me, you have not even the slightest regard for my feelings. But don't think, Mr. Higginson, that I will be treated so any longer; you may break my heart,—your poor Margaret's heart,—if you will, but—but—" And here the affectionate creature was so overcome that she could not utter another word, but sat down wringing her hands and weeping as if I had broken her heart, and she had not crushed my foot! But, as far as my experience enables me to form any opinion on such a subject, I must say, that wives have an extraordinary knack at turning the tables on their husbands.

"For Heaven's sake, madam," said I, "don't set me distracted;"—the pain and her absurd reproaches together made me both frantic and ferocious— "don't make me believe that Adam's wife was made out of the bone of a gouty leg, instead of a good sound rib."

"What do you mean by that, sir?" said Mrs. Higginson.

"Only," said I, gritting my teeth, "that I have some thoughts she must have been a piece of the sorest bone in his body."

My wife marched up to the bed, and looked me in the face. My wrath went out like a gas-light before a black frost; my agonies again disappeared. There was no standing that look, unless one could stand the look of a Jersey black-snake, famous beyond all other snakes for its powers of fascination. And, talking of snakes, I must add, that, while my wife gave me that look, I felt as if one, just turned out of winter-quarters, horribly cold and creepy, were slipping down my back. She looked at me with mingled anger and disdain.

"How often have I told you, Mr. Higginson," she said, "never to attempt to be witty, since you only expose your folly—I won't use any harder word. And whatever you do, sir," she added, beginning to cry again, "don't make a jest of your wife, sir. You're always doing it, sir; you're always making me appear ridiculous to your friends and to myself; you treat me as if I were a fool—you—"

"Madam," said I, endeavouring to appease her a little, for I was quite overcome by her violence, "remember that I have the gout, and am suffering the—"

"Yes!" she cried; "and you are determined that everybody else shall suffer as well as yourself, and me in particular. Oh, Mr. Higginson! how can you use me so? I'll never speak to you another word!"

And down she sat again, weeping and wringing her hands harder than ever, and moping and whining the Lord knows how long.

"Sheppard Lee! Sheppard Lee!" I muttered (but I took good care not to mutter aloud), "you were not the most miserable dog in the world by a great deal. A gouty constitution and a perverse wife are—oh! pangs and purgatory!"

I hoped my consort, being so greatly incensed, would take herself out of the room, when I determined, though it should cost me a howl for every step, to get up and lock the door on her, come of it what might; but she was not of that mind. She maintained her seat, sobbing and sighing, and, by taking off her hat and flinging it pettishly into a corner, made it manifest that she had determined to nurse me in earnest, though in a way entirely of her own. Happily, the paroxysm of suffering, which was at its height when she entered, soon subsided; and being left greatly exhausted, and her sobs having somewhat of a soporific quality, I managed, notwithstanding my mental disquiet, to fall fast asleep; whereby I got rid for a time of an evil in many respects equal to the gout itself.

Two days after I was able to leave my bed, though not to walk: had I been, I am strongly of opinion I should have walked out of my house— out of the city of Philadelphia—and perhaps out of the United States of America—nay, and upon a pinch, out of the world itself, to get rid of my beloved wife. Who would have believed in our village, that John H. Higginson, who seemed to have nothing in the world to do but to slaughter woodcocks, beat his dog Ponto, and ride about in a fine new barouche with a pair of horses that cost a thousand dollars; who had a dwelling-house in Chestnut-street, a brewery in the Northern Liberties, with an ale-butt as big as the basin of the Mediterranean, a goodly store of real estate in town and country, bank-stock and coal-mines, and a thousand other of the good things of the world—who, I say, would have believed that this same John H. Higginson was decidedly the most miserable dog in the whole universe? It was truth, every word of it; and before I was six days old in my new body, I wished—no, not that the devil had me—but I was more than willing he should have the better half of me. I had the gout, my wife was a shrew, and I was—a henpecked husband.

Yes! the reader may stare, and bless his stars—the manly John H. Higginson, who seemed to have no earthly care or trouble, and who was so little deficient in spirit that he could quarrel with a Jersey farmer while trespassing on his grounds, shoot his bull-dog, and take aim at his negro, had long since succumbed to the superior spirit, and acknowledged the irresponsible supremacy of his wife; in the field, and at a distance from his house, he was a man of spirit and figure, but at home the most submissive of the henpecked. Resistance against a petticoat government is, as all know, the most hopeless of resistance: a single man has often subverted a monarchy, and overturned a republic; but history has not yet recorded an instance of successful rebellion on the part of a married man against the tyranny of a wife. The tongue of woman is the only true sceptre; for, unlike other emblems of authority, it is both the instrument of power and the axe of execution. John H. Higginson attempted no resistance against the rule of his wife; the few explosions of impatience of which he was now and then guilty, were punished with a rigour that awed him into discretion. On this subject I feel myself eloquent, and I could expatiate on it by the hour. But I am writing not so much the history of my reflections as of my adventures; and I must hasten on with my story.

CHAPTER VII.

A COMPARISON BETWEEN DUNNING AND SCOLDING, WITH SOME THOUGHTS ON SUICIDE.

No one but a henpecked husband who may happen to be shut up in prison with his wife, can appreciate the horror of the situation in which I now found myself placed. The gout prevented my escaping, even for a moment, from the sway of my spouse; she truly had me tied to her apron-string, and, as I may say, by a cord that went round my sore foot. I was a martyr to two of the greatest ills that ever afflicted a son of Adam; and the two together were not to be borne. Either, if alone, I might perhaps have tolerated, in consideration of the many good things that marked my lot. I might have endured the gout, if I had had a wife who, instead of scolding at me, would have suffered me, as a good wife should, to do all the scolding myself; or I might even have submitted to the tyranny of my Margaret, had I been able to beat a retreat when I grew tired of it. But my wife and the gout together were not to be borne by any human being: they set me, after a while, quite distracted.

What pleasure had I in being the rich John H. Higginson? It was in vain that my brother-in-law, Tim (who, it appears, was the junior partner and factotum in the brewery, as well as manager-general of my affairs), bragged to me of the astonishing rise in my property, and declared I was already worth a hundred thousand dollars; in the midst of my exultation I heard my wife's voice on the stairs, and my joy oozed out of the hair of my head. I could only look at Tim and groan, and Tim did the same; for, poor fellow, though only her brother, he was as much henpecked as myself. "Never mind," said Tim, consolatorily; "your foot will be well by-and-by, and then we shall have a jolly time together." But my comforter took great care on such occasions to sneak out of the house in good time, and so leave me to bear the evil by myself.

In the course of two weeks, or thereabouts, my foot had so far recovered that I was able to put it on the ground, and hobble about a little with a crutch; but I had lost all hope of ever being able to resume my exercises in the field. I was therefore reduced to despair; and my wife becoming more intolerable every day, I began to be so weary of existence, that I was once or twice on the point of making away with myself.

She was, in truth, the nonpareil of women and of scolders. I have called her a shrew; but it must not be supposed she was of that species to which men give the name of Tartar. She was none of your fierce, pepper-tempered creatures, who wrangle in a loud voice over the whole house, and sometimes take broomsticks to the servants. Such viragoes are in a measure sufferable, for they are sometimes in a good-humour. My Margaret was of the family of *Croakers*, as they are called; that is, of a lugubrious, grumbling complexion, always sad and whining, full of suspicions and reproaches, now in tears, now in hysterics, always in an ill-humour, and so keeping every one about her in a state of misery. I never knew a servant, male or female, old or young, black or white, to remain in the house two weeks at a time, except a poor little negress that had been bound to me—that is, my prototype—under indentures; and she, after running away a dozen times, began to mope, and pine, and look so sorrowful, that, out of pity, I sent her home to her mother. As for myself, being incapable of flying, and exposed all day long to her lectures and reproaches, I became melancholy and desperate, wished myself Sheppard Lee again, with the constable and sheriff both after me, and, twice or thrice, as I have hinted before, resolved to put an end to my life.

One day, while I was reading the papers, I fell upon the account of a man who had hanged himself. "He was in good circumstances," said the journal, "and had a wife and three children. No reason has been assigned or suspected for his rash act."

"No doubt his wife was a shrew!" said I to myself, "and there was no way of getting rid of her; and so it was the wisest thing the poor man could do."

I thought over this occurrence so long, that it produced a great effect upon my mind; and my wife leaving me one day more incensed and desperate than ever, I snatched up a bit of cord that lay in my way, and resolved to strangle myself forthwith. I should have hanged myself over the chamber door, but was in dread I might slip down to the floor, and hurt my foot; and thinking it more genteel to die in my bed, I made the cord into a noose, or ring, through which, having placed it about my neck, I clapped a silver candlestick, by means of which I thought I might twist the cord tight enough to strangle me. And so I might, had I possessed the nerve; but in truth, I no sooner found my breath a little obstructed, than I became alarmed with the idea of apoplexy, which was always frightful to me, and so gave over my purpose.

On another occasion I sent to an apothecary whom I knew, for a vial of prussic acid, which takes life so expeditiously, that, as I supposed, one could have no time to be in pain. But that I might know in what manner it operated, I gave a quantity to a neighbour's cat, which had found her way into my chamber, and made friends with me during my confinement; and the creature was thrown into such horrible convulsions, and set up such a diabolical yell, that although she was stone-dead in less than half a minute, I was convinced this was the most uncomfortable way of dying that could be hit on.

I had then some thoughts of drowning myself, and only hesitated whether I should try the experiment in the bath-tub, or wait until I could bear a ride over the paving-stones to the river. As to cutting my throat, or blowing my brains out, I had never the slightest idea of trying either; for in respect to the former, besides that it makes such a horrible puddle of blood about one's body, it causes one to look as vulgar and low-lived as a slaughtered bullock; and as for the latter, I was so familiar with fire-arms, that I knew them to be weapons one cannot trifle with.

But fortune, that had served me such a scurvy trick in saddling me with gout and a scolding wife, along with the wealth of John H. Higginson, willed that I should employ none of these deadly expedients against my life, but get rid of my distresses in a manner much more remarkable and novel.

CHAPTER VIII.

SHEPPARD LEE FORMS SUNDRY ACQUAINTANCES, SOME OF WHICH ARE GENTEEL.

It was three full weeks before I left my chamber; and during the last days of that confinement, the only amusement I had consisted in looking from the window, after properly poising my leg on a soft cushion, upon what passed in the streets; and this, as the reader may suppose, I only enjoyed when my wife left off tormenting me for a moment, to go down stairs and torment the servants.

This was poor pastime for one of my habits and turn of mind; but my wife had made me contemplative; and had it not been for the perpetual dread of her return that I was under, I think I might have extracted some diversion from what I saw in the streets. But being in constant fear and vexation, I looked on with a spirit too morose and cynical for my own enjoyment.

Day after day, between the hours of five and six in the afternoon, I observed Mr. Cutclose, the tailor, descend from his marble steps, and climb upon the back of a horse, to take the evening air. He rode like one who had taken his chief lessons on the shop-board; and I often wondered he did not draw up his legs, and sit on the saddle hunker-fashion at once; but what particularly struck me was the compliment he paid himself of wearing his own coats, cut American-fashion about the arm-holes, and so keeping himself in purgatory all day long. He used to give parties every fortnight, and invite all the dandies whom he had down in his tick-book; by which means his entertainments were rendered highly genteel and fashionable.

Next door to Mr. Cutclose lived the great lawyer of our square, the celebrated Coke Butterside, Esq. I could see him sally out every morning with his green bag, which he carried in his own hands, either because he intended to be a candidate at the next Congressional election, and would seem democratic, or because he was afraid, if he intrusted it to another, the devil might snap it up as his own property. He had a lordly, self-satisfied air about him, as if he felt the full merit of his vocation, and prided himself upon having more men by the ears than any other in the whole city. His bow was exceedingly condescending, and his look protecting.

Nearer at hand was the dwelling of the old note-shaver—old Goldfist, as they called him, though his true name was Skinner. He was horribly rich, and such a miserly, insatiable old hunks, that although he had ostensibly retired from business (he was originally a pawn-broker) for some six or seven years, he still kept up his trade in a certain way, that was not so reputable as gainful, and of which I shall have occasion to say something by-and-by. He was said to be a good friend of such desperate young gentlemen as moved in high life, and had passable expectations from rich uncles and parents, but he was said to hold his friendship at very extortionate prices. How such a skinflint as he ever came to live in a good house and in a fashionable quarter, was a question not easy to solve. But according to Tim my brother-in-law's story, he came for economy, having got the house of a demolished aristocrat who had fallen into his clutches, and found it in so dilapidated a condition that he chose to live in it himself rather than submit to the expense of preparing it for a tenant. It brought him, moreover, nearer to his customers; and perhaps the old curmudgeon, who had a daughter and a brace of hopeful sons, had a hope of thus getting them into society.

But one who lives at Heaven's gate does not live in Heaven, as the saying is. Old Goldfist kept neither horses nor carriages, nor did he give parties: I doubt whether he ever asked anybody to dine with him in his life; and as for his boys and his girl, all of whom were grown up, he kept them in such a mean condition that they were not company for genteel people. Everybody despised them, especially Cutclose the tailor, who turned up his nose at them, and called them *rooterers*, which, I am told (for I never troubled myself to study the modern languages, there being so many of them), is a French word signifying *low people*.[1]

This old money-maker, who had a stoop in the shoulders, used to parade the street up and down before his own door every sunshiny day, in a thread-bare brown coat, to which he sometimes added a blue spencer roundabout, a silver-headed stick in one hand, and a yellow handkerchief in the other. The latter he was wont every two or three minutes to clap to his nose, producing thereby an explosion, which, notwithstanding the muffler over his nostrils, was prodigiously strong and sonorous; and once, to my knowledge, it frightened a young lady into the gutter.

I could say a great deal more of this old gentle man, whom everybody despised, but whom every man took off his hat to, on account of his wealth; but I shall have occasion to speak of him hereafter.

As for the rest of my neighbours, I do not think them worthy of notice. I might, indeed, except Mr. Periwinkle Smith, my opposite neighbour, spoken of before, whom I knew to belong to that order of aristocracy which is emphatically termed chip-chop, and who was of such pure blood that it had known no mechanical taint for three different generations, the nearest approach to such disgrace being found in a family of ragamuffins, who claimed to be Mr. Smith's relations, merely because they were descended from his grandfather, but who were very properly discountenanced by him.

This old gentleman had a daughter who seemed to be universally admired, judging from the numbers of visiters of both sexes who besieged her father's door every morning. To do her justice, I must say she was very handsome; but she had the additional merit of being an only child, and therefore an heiress, as was supposed. I thought so myself, until Tim, who knew something of everybody's affairs, assured me that her father's estate was eaten up by mortgages, that he was poor as a rat, and would die insolvent.

Among the many young gentlemen who paid court to the fair Miss Smith, I noticed one, who, besides being more assiduous in his attentions, seemed also to enjoy a greater share of her regard than others. He was a young fellow of uncommonly genteel figure; that is, he was long and lank, somewhat narrow in the shoulders, but clean-limbed, and straight as an arrow. He had a long face and hollow cheeks; but what his jaws lacked in flesh was made up to them in beard, his whiskers, which were coal-black, being as exuberant as if made by a brush-maker, and stretching from his temples to the point of his chin, and so enveloping his whole face. He had besides a pair of peaked mustaches, that would have done honour to the Grand Seignior; and, with a turban and caftan on, he might have paid his respects to the alumni of any college in the land, without even the necessity of speaking bad Latin.[2] He dressed well, walked with a step as easy and majestical as a stork or an ostrich, and was evidently a favourite with the ladies.

His name, Tim told me, was I. D.—that is to say, Isaac Dulmer—Dawkins; though, in consideration of the rusticalness of the first member of the triad, and from regard to his feelings, which were outraged by its pronunciation, his friends had universally agreed to suppress it; and, in consequence, he was called I. Dulmer Dawkins, Esquire, that title being added, because it is the only one an American gentleman not in office, or the militia, can claim. He was, as Timothy assured me, a dandy of the true style, being a born scion of the chip-chop order, and, as such, admitted to all its honours and immunities, though without the support of any living relations in society, or, as his ill luck would have it, of connexions either. He was said to possess some little property in town, and, what was still better, to be the heir of a rich uncle without children, whom he expected to die within a reasonable period. As for his town property, my brother Tim doubted its existence altogether, and would perhaps have been as skeptical in regard to the uncle, had he not known that an uncle did really exist, and a rich one too, for he was largely concerned in the distilling and lumbering business on the Susquehanna.

I am particular in making the reader acquainted with Mr. I. Dulmer Dawkins, inasmuch as it was my fortune, after a time, to fall into a connexion with him myself—as intimate as it was unexpected.

When I first saw him, I accounted him an ugly and uncouth personage, and I regarded him with contempt and dislike. I had acquired, along with other peculiarities of John H. Higginson, a hearty hatred for all people who considered themselves better than myself; for, rich and respectable as I was, I soon perceived that I was considered a very low, vulgar personage by the true chip-chop aristocracy, and I longed greatly at times, as I looked out of the window upon them, to take some of them by the ears, and settle the matter of superiority between us in that way.

But as for Mr. Dulmer Dawkins, I soon began to experience an interest in him, which was indeed of a somewhat envious complexion. I frequently saw him dancing along at the side of the fair Miss Smith; and he seemed so exceedingly happy and content, and she cast upon him so many approving glances, that I could not help contrasting his condition with mine. There he strutted in the open street, young, active, and hale, as ignorant of disease as of care, and here sat I, in a sick chamber, imprisoned with the gout. There he moved at the side of a young and elegant woman, who eyed him with admiration, doubtless, also, with regard, and who had such native amiableness and cheerfulness imprinted together on her countenance, that it was plain she must prove a blessing, rather than a curse, to him who should be so happy as to wed her; while I, miserable I! was tied to such a wife as I could scarce have the cruelty to wish bestowed upon my worst enemy, contracted to an ague, married, as I may say, to a toothache. I should have been glad to exchange conditions with Mr. Dulmer Dawkins— ay, by my honour! if there was ever honour in man—or with anybody else.

From Tim's account it seemed that my young gentleman had a longer face than head; in other words, that nature had endowed him more bountifully with beard than brains: and, in truth, I judged, by the way he showed his teeth and rolled his eyes at the fair Miss Smith, and a thousand other little grimaces and affectations I was witness to, that he was neither more wise nor brilliant than the others of his tribe. But what of that? Wisdom and care go hand in hand, and wit makes us uncomfortable: fools are the only happy people. So I used to think, while I looked on Mr. I. D. Dawkins and the fair Miss Smith.

But it is an ill way to pass time, peeping into millstones, or reading men's history out of their faces. Dulmer Dawkins had his cares, as well as another. I suddenly missed him from the street; the fair Miss Smith made her promenades, attended by other admirers, and for three whole days Mr. Dawkins was invisible. On the fourth he reappeared: I saw him as he came up the street, escorting another belle, entirely unknown to me, but of a dashing appearance. As he passed Mr. Periwinkle Smith's house, the fair Miss Smith issued from the door. Mr. Dawkins made her a low and most elegant bow, his companion waved her fan, and they passed on, looking unutterable things at one another. The fair Miss Smith seemed confounded; a flush appeared on her face, and then vanished; she looked after her admirer, and then, with her attendants, two young coxcombs who were with her, descended the steps, and walked down the street. I saw her once turn her head half round as if to look again after Dulmer; but her curiosity, anger, sorrow, or whatever feeling it was prompted the movement, was restrained, and she strode off at an unusually rapid and unfashionable gait. "So, so! my turtles have been quarrelling," I said to myself; "and the fair Miss Smith is just a Jezebel, like the rest of her confounded sex!"—It never occurred to me to think a quarrel arising between two persons of different sexes could be caused by any thing but the unreasonable behaviour of the lady.

It was two weeks before I saw Dulmer Dawkins again, and then I beheld him under a new aspect.

[1] Perhaps *roturiers*. Rooterers is, however, good America French — Printer's Devil.

[2] Here Sheppard Lee seems to have had in his eye a very ingenious loafer of Pearl Slip, or thereabouts who, some years since, was seized with the whim of travelling, and bamboozling the politic, especially the learned part thereof. By the aid of little dog-Latin, horribly anglicized in idiom and pronunciation, a stock of Gothamic impudence, and features truly Yankee and vernacular, he convinced the cognoscenti of one or more learned institutions that he was a highly unlucky son of a Turk, born all the way off at Damascus.

CHAPTER IX.

THE AUTHOR GROWS WEARY OF HIS WIFE, AND MISTAKES THE SCHUYLKILL FOR THE RIVER LETHE.—THE TRAGICAL ADVENTURE THAT BEFELL A YOUNG GENTLEMAN IN THAT ROMANTIC TIDE, WITH ITS EFFECTS UPON THE DESTINIES OF SHEPPARD LEE.

It may be supposed, since I was able to amuse my mind with such observations, that they detracted from the miseries of my condition, or at least assuaged in some measure my pangs. But as well might one believe that the condemned malefactor, who looks out from his cart on the volunteer companies escorting him to the gallows, and admires the splendid incoherence of their trappings—their infantry coats and horsemen's hats, their republican faces and imperial colours—feels thereby less dissatisfaction with his shroud and coffin, and the rope coiled so inelegantly round his neck. My observations were made only at intervals that were both brief and rare. My wife was the most attentive creature that ever set a husband distracted; and under the plea of nursing me, gave me so much of her company, that I was gradually driven to desperation. In course of time I was happily able to get into my barouche, and thus, for a short hour or two, escape my tormentor. Had that period been deferred a week later, I should certainly have taken an ounce of arsenic that I found lying in a closet, though I knew it was awful bad stuff to swallow.

As soon as I found myself once more at liberty, I began to con over a project I had formed of deserting my dear Margaret altogether; and this I resolved to put into execution the moment my foot should be well enough for travelling. But, oh horror! just as the doctor pronounced me cured, I was seized with a second paroxysm, and beheld nothing before me but eternal captivity and unmitigated wife!

This attack was brought on by the mere triumph of restoration. The afternoon before, I drove out upon the Schuylkill, with Tim and another friend; and several other jolly dogs meeting us, we stopped together at a well-known house of entertainment on the banks of that river, and resolved to enjoy ourselves. I declare in all sincerity that I was very moderate both in eating and drinking; but having sat at the table until after nightfall, and being well content to tarry longer, I made a sudden and rash resolution not to return that night at all, nor upon the following day either, if I could avoid it. But as it was necessary to account for my absence to my wife, I instructed Tim to tell her I had contracted a sudden fit of podagra, which made it proper I should not expose myself to the night-air. With this fib in his mouth, Tim, who considered the whole thing a capital joke, as indeed he did every other of my devising, returned to the city, whither he was followed by the others before midnight.

Now whether it was that the immoderate satisfaction I indulged in, at enjoying even a few hours of quiet, was an excess capable of bringing on a paroxysm of gout,—whether it was the unwholesome night-air of the Schuylkill, so famous for its agues and bilious fevers, or whether indeed it was not the lie I had invented, which was punished upon me in the reality of the affliction I had assumed,—it is certain that I woke up the next morning in quite a feverish condition, and with all the symptoms of returning podagra, though I did not immediately suspect it. It was not until towards nightfall that I understood my situation.

In the meanwhile Tim had returned, and again driven back to town without me, to assure my affectionate spouse, that, being entirely recovered, I thought it best to defer my return until the evening; at which time I proposed to be sick again, so as to excuse my remaining from home a second night. In this way I designed to put off my return from night till morning, and from morning till night, as long as I could.

Feeling a little better about dinner-time, I indulged in a hearty meal, and then lay down. But I had not slept many hours before I dreamed the devil was tugging at my foot with a pair of red-hot tongs; and starting up in anguish, I perceived clearly enough that my malady had returned.

"Miserable wretch that I am!" I cried; "why was I not content to be Sheppard Lee? Was poverty worse than the gout? was debt equal in torment to a scolding wife? What a fool I was to change my condition.— Would that I was now a dog!"

I hobbled down to the porch of the inn, not without pain, for my foot was awfully tender, and began to picture to myself the misery that was inevitably prepared for me. The thought of living a month longer in the same house with my wife, entirely at her mercy, drove me to despair; in the midst of which, being roused by the sound of approaching wheels, I looked up, and beheld my wife herself, advancing as fast as my elegant bays could bear her, to pay me a visit. I knew her by her white feathers, and my brother Tim was sitting at her side.

At this sight my philosophy forsook me altogether; I fell into a phrensy, and disregarding the condition of my foot, or rather sharpened and confirmed in my purpose by the pangs it gave me, I rushed down to the river-side towards a spot where I knew there was deep water, resolved to throw myself in without a moment's delay; and this without considering that, as it was hot weather, I should spoil the water drunk by my fellow-citizens. This was an objection that partly occurred to me before, when debating the subject of drowning; and I think it so serious a one, that I would recommend to the councils of Philadelphia to appoint a bailiff, whose express duty should be to prevent people drowning themselves in the basin; and the same person might have an eye to the drowned cats, dogs, pigs, calves, dead fish, and swimming boys, that somewhat detract from the agreeableness of the water.

I reached the place just as the barouche drew up at the door, and hopping forward, I began to slip off my coat and waistcoat, and draw out my watch and pocketbook, though for what purpose, I am sure I cannot say. But what was my surprise to perceive myself forestalled in my intentions by another person, who stood upon the very rock from which I designed to throw myself, and was evidently preparing to exercise justice upon himself in the same summary way. He was a tall, lank personage, of highly genteel figure and habit; but his back being towards me, I could not see his face.

I had scarce laid eyes upon him before, with a very violent motion of his arm, he cast his hat into the stream, and immediately afterward his neck-cloth; then slapping his hands together like one who is about rushing into a fight, and rushing into it with resolution, he exclaimed, "The devil take all women and tailors!" and leaped into the river, which instantly closed over his head.

I was so petrified at his rashness that I forgot my own, and stood staring on the water, as it came rushing in agitated ripples to the shore, lost in such confusion and horror, that for a space of a minute or more I neither moved hand nor foot. The water, which, previous to the plunge, had been as smooth as a mirror, was fast regaining its tranquillity, when, on a sudden, a great bubbling began to appear a few yards below the rock, and I saw the top of a man's head come to the surface, and immediately after sink again.

At that sight, my presence of mind was restored; and being much concerned that a young fellow, as he appeared to be, should perish so miserably, I rushed into the river, and being a good diver, had but little trouble to fish him up, and drag him to the shore. But I pulled him out a moment too late; he was as dead as a herring, or appeared to be; for his countenance was distorted, and blue as an in digo-bag, and his mouth full of foam; a circumstance which I regretted the more, as I no sooner looked him in the face than I recognised the features of my friend, if I may so call him, Mr. I. Dulmer Dawkins.

As I was dragging the body to the shore, a carriage came rattling along the road, which is there so near to the river that those who were in it could easily perceive the act in which I was engaged, and they stopped it to give me assistance. It was at that very moment that I discovered who it was I was carrying; and I was so much surprised at the discovery, that I cried out in a loud voice, "I. D. Dawkins, by the Lord!"

There was immediately a great screaming in the carriage, and out rushed my aristocratical neighbour, Mr. Periwinkle Smith, with two young ladies, one of whom was his daughter; and such an uproar and lamentation as they made about me, were perhaps never before made by so small a number of genteel people, on any occasion. I was particularly affected by the expressions of the fair Miss Smith, who seemed overcome by grief; and, as I did not doubt she had an affection for the young fellow, I wondered what folly could have driven him into this act of suicide.

But my wonder was not very long-lived; the cries of the two ladies had reached the inn, and drawn every soul therein to the scene of disaster. They came running towards us, and I saw that my wife was among them.

I could maintain my equanimity no longer: in the bitterness of my heart I muttered, almost aloud, and as sincerely as I ever muttered any thing in my life, "I would I were this addle-pate Dawkins, were it only to be lying as much like a drowned rat as he!"

I had not well grumbled the last word, before a sudden fire flashed before my eyes, a loud noise like the roar of falling water passed through my head, and I lost all sensation and consciousness.

***

BOOK III.
CONTAINING MUCH THAT WILL BE INTERESTING TO YOUNG GENTLEMEN IN DEBT, AND TO FATHERS OF FAMILIES WHO DESIRE TO HAVE THEIR CHILDREN RISE IN SOCIETY.

CHAPTER I.

THE FIRST CHAPTER OF THE HISTORY OF I. D. DAWKINS, ESQ.

When I recovered my wits, I thought I had got into the place which is never mentioned among polite people, except at church. I perceived a horrible smell of gin, whiskey, hartshorn, tobacco-smoke, and spirits of camphire, as if these made up the constituents of the atmosphere of darkness; and I saw, though very obscurely, for the light was dim, and there seemed to be films over my eyes, a number of figures that moved to and fro, uttering discordant noises. One of them, it seems, and I took it for granted he was the chief devil, stood by me, pressing my ribs with a fist that felt marvellously heavy, while with the other he maintained a grasp upon my nose, to which ever and anon he gave a considerable tweak; while another, little less dreadful, stood at his side, armed with some singular weapon, shaped much like a common fire-bellows, the nozle of which he held at but a little distance from my own. There were four others of them, each of whom had me by a leg or arm, pulling and slapping with much zeal, and, as I supposed, preparing me for a gridiron; while divers others flitted about, as I mentioned before, talking with voices that appeared to me louder than thunder.

Such were the observations which I made, vaguely and confusedly (for there was a great stupor over most of my senses), and which led me to suspect I was in the place of torment; in which suspicion I was confirmed by a thousand pangs I felt all over my body, so strange, racking, and horrible, that unless one were to have the toothache, gout, earache, gravel, rheumatism, headache, a stumped toe, and locked jaw all together, it would be impossible to form any just conception of the nature and variety of my torments. I had, I verily believed, the paddle-wheel of a steamboat in my head, which was revolving full thirty times a minute, with a hideous crashing and clamour, and churning my brains to atoms; and, by the same rule, I conceived there was an iron-foundry in my lungs and heart, every cell and cavity of which was full of hot castings.

But it would require a greater space than the subject is worthy of, to describe the agonies I endured in those moments of torture; and they were, perhaps, the more poignant, since I could neither move a muscle, nor vent my distresses in a single cry,—which I was the more inclined to do from conceiving myself in the kingdom of darkness.

When I opened my eyes, I heard him who had me by the nose yell out something to the others; upon which there was a great stir and outcry among them, and I distinctly heard one say, after a great oath, "We'll do well enough without a doctor."

"What!" said I to myself, "have they doctors here too? Do they follow their patients?"

"But," continued the same voice, "we'll never finish the job till we roll him over a barrel. He'll never show game till the water's out of him."

These words, it may be supposed, were sufficient to give my mind the right cue, and relieve me of all apprehensions in relation to death and condemnation. On the contrary, they confirmed me the more strongly in my conceit. How there should be water in me I knew not; but my idea was, the inhuman imps wished to roll it out of me, only to make me burn the better. Fortunately for me, another voice made answer, and opposed the atrocious proposal.

"No rolling on barrels," it said, "nor hanging up by the heels"—(hanging up by the heels! thought I)—"it is against the rules of the Humane Society; and here they are."

"The Humane Society!" thought I; "is there a Humane Society among the devils?"

"The rule is," the second voice went on, "as soon as the body shows signs of life, snaps its eyes, and breathes, to pour a little brandy and water down."

"Brandy and water!" said the first voice, evidently in a passion; "and I wonder if that a'n't against the rules of the Temperance Society? Better give the man so much burning brimstone?"

"The Temperance Society?" thought I.—I might have brought myself to believe they had a Temperance Society, as well as a Humane one, in the lower regions, had it not been for the violent ardour of him who pronounced its name. I knew by his rage and fury he could belong to no Temperance Society but in the United States of America; and the inference was therefore plain, that instead of being in the other world, I was in the United States of America myself.

But before I could infer myself into this happy belief, I was confused by a hot argument that grew up between the advocates of the two societies, who waxed quarrelsome, until there was a sudden cry, "The doctor has come!" which pacified them in a moment, and satisfied me I was neither dead nor buried.

The doctor stalked up to me; I thought I knew his features and voice, but my sight and hearing were still confused. I have no doubt he treated me *secundum artem*; but in about five minutes I was as dead as ever.

CHAPTER II.

A CONVERSATION BETWIXT THE AUTHOR AND HIS BOSOM FRIEND, JOHN TICKLE, ESQ.

———

However, it was not my fate to die in good earnest. By-and-by I opened my eyes, feeling in very passable health, though somewhat weak and dejected.

The devils, or my late attendants, whoever they were, had all vanished, and with them noise, darkness, and the various ill odours that had afflicted my nostrils. I was lying in a very good bed, and chamber with curtained windows, the curtains being closed, to keep out the sunshine that was playing on them; and at my side there sat in an arm-chair a young gentleman of a buckish appearance, sound asleep. The creaking of the bed, as I rose on my elbow, roused him; he started, rubbed his eyes, and, looking me in the face, burst into a hearty laugh.

"Bravo!" he cried; "I told old Boneset so! I could watch as comfortably as ever a child's nurse of Messina. I thought I should have the child wake me with crying! I vow to gad, I've been snoozing all night. And so you've opened your peepers like an honest man at last, Dawky!—Pray, what the devil made you drown yourself?"

And here the young gentleman, seizing me by the hand, fell a laughing again, and that with more zest than before.

"Sah!" said I, looking at him with both surprise and confusion; for, though his voice and face seemed familiar to me, I could not for the life of me say who he was. "Sa—ah, really I—ah—" and here I stopped; for, first, I knew not what to say, and secondly, my bewildered looks set him into such a roar of merriment, that there was no saying a word to him.

"Come, you dog," said he, with a grin here and a roar there, "don't be comical just after coming out of the grave. A man just fished out of a river, and rescued from death after a hard fight between the doctor and the devil, should be serious and ecclesiastical, solemn of visage, and sanctified of conversation. No joking, you dog; but get up, Absalomize, and talk. No joking, I say; no joking with Jack Tickle."

As he spoke he seized me by the shoulder, and dragged me half out of bed.

"Ged and demmee!" said I, "remember my foot!" For my toe catching in the bed-cord, I suddenly recollected the gouty member.

"I will," said he, with another roar; "for, the Lord knows, 'tis the best part of you. Spoil Dawky's foot, and ruin him with women and shoe-makers for ever! The one ceases to adore, and the other trusts no longer."

"But I mean the gout," said I.

"The fiddlestick and fiddle!" said he: "whoever heard of a poor dandy, living on tick, having the gout? Up, Dawky, my dog, and tell me what set you to drowning? If 'twas about Betty Small, 'twas a small matter. What! drown for being jilted! If 'twas about the tailor's bill, 'twas still more ridiculous. I say, Dawky, my fellow, *what* made you drown yourself?"

"Drown myself!" said I; but I said it with a stare. The odd behaviour and expressions of the young gentleman, who called himself Jack Tickle (a name that I never remembered to have heard before in my life, although his countenace was certainly highly familiar), and certain queer associations his appearance gave birth to; the singularity of my feelings; and, more than all, the appearance of my foot and leg (the former of which, instead of being tumid and red with gout, was white, and of elegant shape, while the latter, which but the day before had a calf to compare with any old Quaker's in Arch-street, was now as lank as a sword-blade); I say, these circumstances had the effect to increase my confusion to that degree, that I felt like one who is asleep and knows it—provided one ever did or can feel so.

In the midst of all I suddenly cast my eyes upon a goodly large looking-glass that hung against the wall, and saw my reflection therein. It was the image of Mr. I. Dulmer Dawkins! his exact representation, perfect in beard and visage, save that the former was in great disorder, and the latter somewhat white, and equally perfect in figure, as far as I could compare a man in buff and linen to one in the full panoply of the tailor.

"My ged!" said I, "I am transformed again!"

And with that I made a hop up to the glass to look at myself closer. There was no mistaking the matter, even if the looking-glass had. I looked at my legs, and I gave a tweak at my mustaches. My shoulders were elegantly narrow, and my foot as sound as a savage's. I jumped up, cut a pigeon-wing, and then, descending, attempted a ballet-dancer's pirouette; after which I looked again into the glass. I was a young man of twenty-five, and the most elegant fellow I ever laid eyes on!

I ran to Jack, and hugged him round the neck, crying, "Lard, Jack, you rogue, I'm the most comical creature that ever lived!"

"Ay," said he, smothering with laughter and my embraces together; "but what made you drown yourself?"

I recollected all about it, and suddenly felt astonished. I remembered how I had jumped into the water, and how I had fished myself out, as dead as a poker; that is, how Mr. Higginson had fished me, or rather how I had fished Mr. Dawkins. I remembered how I, John Hazlewood Higginson, had wished to be Mr. I. Dulmer Dawkins, and now I was Mr. I. Dulmer Dawkins himself, and nobody but he. I sat down on the bedside, marvelling how such a thing could be; and the wonder of it was indeed amazing. That my spirit should creep into a man's body, though strange enough, was not so prodigiously surprising; but that my spirit and body together (for I did not know it had been otherwise disposed of), especially so corpulent a one as John H. Higginson's, should get into one—that was truly marvellous.

But my study was brought to an end by Tickle suddenly exclaiming, with a voice of concern, "Curse him! gad, poor fellow, I believe he has washed his wits out! He has gone mad!"

"No more than you have," said I, shaking him by the hand; "but you must allow it is a most extraordinary affair."

"'Pon honour, yes," said he, laughing as hard as ever; "but what made you throw yourself into the river?"

"Why," said I, in a hurry, "to save Dawkins."

"To save Dawkins!!!" said he, looking at me as one would look at a shoemaker who brings a pair of shoes home the day he has promised them.

"That is," said I, "to save Higginson."

"To save Higginson!!!" he cried, with such a roar of laughter as made my teeth rattle; "why there were twenty people saw Higginson drag *you* out! I say, Dawky, no lillibullering—what did you jump into the river for?"

"I jumped," said I, quite in a quandary, "after my hat."

At this answer my friend Jack Tickle threw himself upon the bed, where he rolled over and over, until his coat was covered with down and feathers, which cooled his transports a little.

"I see," said he, "I see! It was the last of the family; for hatters' tick was exhausted! Right, Dawky; in such straits of credit, I think I should have jumped after mine! Who would not fight, roast, or drown, for his hat, when it was the last decent one he ever expected to have on his head? I am glad *this* was the cause: it makes me think better of you. I thought, like the rest, it was on account of your disappointment from the adorable Betty—"

"The devil take Betty!" said I, but without well knowing why.

"He *has!*" cried Jack, uproariously; "at least a *poor* devil has. She has thrown away her seventy thousand upon a fellow no more to be compared with you than a tame goose with a wild one: and instead of spending it like a man, the rascal will buy stocks, and save it. I say, Dawky, you must have been surprised at her conduct—as we all were;—really, we thought you had her; and there was no one more certain than the fair Miss Smith."

"The devil take the fair Miss Smith!" said I.

"He will," said Tickle, shaking his head and laughing; "or, if *he* don't, I don't know who will; for it is a clear matter—dad's done up entirely, and they say the sheriff is already making an inventory of his chattels. A great pity, Dawky; for, if she had but money, Miss Smith would be certainly an angel incarnate—a nymph, a houri—the finest woman in town. I say, Dawky, I think she almost had you!"

CHAPTER III.

IN WHICH SHEPPARD LEE IS PREPARED FOR THE BRILLIANT DESTINY THAT AWAITS HIM.

———

There were many things in the conversation of my friend Tickle which I did not exactly comprehend, though I had a vague, confused appreciation of all, and afterward understood him well enough. The fact is, I was in the same difficulty which had beset me when scarce warm in the body of Mr. Higginson, that is, a confusion of characters, propensities, and associations, only that the last were imperfect, as if my memory had suddenly given way; and besides, the difficulty was in both cases increased by the feeling of amazement with which, for several hours, when properly conscious of it, I pondered over the marvel of my transformation. How such a thing could happen, or had happened, I knew no more than the man in the moon: it was a new thing in the history of man, and there was nothing in philosophy (at least, such philosophy as I had at that time) to explain it. I had certainly done nothing, on my part, in either case, to effect a change, save merely wishing it; and it seemed to me that I possessed a power, never before known to a human being, of transferring my spirit from body to body, whenever I willed, at least, under certain circumstances. But on this subject I will have more to say hereafter.

Happen how and by what means it might, it was certain a transfer *had* taken place; and that I was no longer the poor miserable John H. Higginson, with the gout and a scolding wife; the conception and full consciousness of which were so rapturous, that I suddenly bounded on my feet, and danced about like a madman, now running to the glass to admire my youthful and elegant appearance, and now flinging my arms round the neck of my friend, and hugging him twenty times over.

The conversation that passed between us was exceedingly joyous and varied; though, as I said before, I had but an imperfect understanding of many things Tickle said; for which reason I will record no more of his expressions, lest they should confuse the reader's mind, as they did mine. Some things, however, I gathered from him in relation to my catastrophe and resuscitation which are proper to be told.

It seems that when I—that is, John H. Higginson—wished I were, or might be, the defunct, Dulmer Dawkins, I fell down under a sudden stroke of apoplexy, which was supposed to be caused by my exertions to rescue the unfortunate beau; and, indeed, I saw in the first newspaper I looked into, upon getting to Philadelphia afterward, a long account of my demise, with a highly eulogistic and affecting account of my heroism in sacrificing my life for another's; for, as the paragraph stated, I was of a full and plethoric habit, strongly inclined to apoplexy, of which I was aware myself, as well as of the danger of over exertion; and therefore my act was the more truly heroic. The paper was of a highly democratic character, and the notice was closed by a ferocious warning to the young bug of aristocracy (meaning the elegant and fashionable. I. Dulmer Dawkins), "to remember, when wasting his trivial existence in that heartless society, whose pleasures were obtained at the expense of their worthier, though poorer fellow-creatures, that the preservation of it had cost the nation one of its most excellent citizens, and the world a virtuous man and pure patriot:"—by which I understood that John H. Higginson was of the democratic party; although that was a circumstance of which the gout and my wife had kept me ignorant, as long as I lived in his body.

As for me—that is, I. D. Dawkins—being lugged into the tavern, along with my late tenement, the body of John H. Higginson, I was fallen foul of by all hands; and what with tweaking my nose, beating my arms, scorching my legs with hot bricks, flaying me with salt, whiskey, spirits, and such things, and filling my lungs with dust and ashes from an old fire-bellows, I was brought to life again, greatly to the triumph of my tormentors, before the appearance of a physician; who, however, subsequently assured me they had revived me with such effect as to give him double trouble to keep me in the land of the living afterward; for it seems, after being more dead than alive all that night, I had remained in a kind of stupor all the following day, from which I awoke on the second morning, well enough, as the doctor prognosticated I would be, but only after I had remained more than thirty-six hours in a state of insensibility.

As for my body—that is, Higginson's—it had the honour, after being cogitated over by the coroner, of riding home in my splendid barouche, with the thousand-dollar hourses; but whether my wife went with it or not, I never cared to inquire. It was enough she was gone; and oh, rapture of raptures! gone for ever.

My friend Tickle illuminated me as to other matters, especially in relation to the fair Miss Smith; with whom, it seems (and I recollected all about it when he had set my new associations properly to work), I had been quite particular, until he himself discovered the insolvency of her father's estate; when (and this I began to recollect in the same manner) I instantly turned my attentions upon another—the fair Miss Small—who jilted me. These things, I say, I soon began to recall to mind, as well as many other incidents in the past life of I. Dulmer Dawkins; and, indeed, in the course of a few days, I was as much at home in his body, and among his affairs, as he had ever been himself. But of this anon. I learned that Mr. Periwinkle Smith, after seeing me lodged in the tavern, had driven off to town to engage medical assistance; and this he did so effectually, that I had no less than seven doctors at one time to send me their bills; which was a very foolish thing of them.

Of these things, I say, I discoursed with my friend Jack Tickle, whose conversation, together with the happy consciousness I had of my transformation, infused inexpressible vivacity into my spirits. I was marvellously pleased at the idea of being a fine young fellow, with the freedom of chip-chop society; and I was impatient to return to the city to enjoy my happiness.

"Bravo!" said Jack; "we'll walk in together. But do you know, Dawky," he went on, nodding and winking, "that this is a cursed no-credit place, and that the man below betrayed a certain vulgar anxiety about scot and lot, and the extra expenses you had put him to? What do you say about paying?"

"Really," said I, clapping my hands into my pockets, "I have forgotten my pocketbook!"

"To be sure you have," said Tickle, laughing; "but why need you tell me so? I am no shop-keeper."

"I mean," said I, in alarm, "demmee, that I have lost it, and with that hundred-dollar bill my brother Tim—"

"Your brother Tim!" said Tickle; "who's he?"

I was struck all aback. I remembered that I was I. D. Dawkins.

Tickle perceived my confusion, and enjoyed it, attributing it to another cause.

"Right!" said he, grinning with delight; "but don't make any pretence with me. I didn't expect you to have any money; and, the Lord be thanked, I have. I'll square your account, my dear fellow, and help you to a pigeon besides."

With these words, and many others not needful to be mentioned, he led the way down stairs, where he became astonishingly grave and dignified—a peculiarity I found myself falling into—slapped his ratan against his legs, called for "his friend Dawkins's bill," and paid it—that is, I suppose he did, for I stalked out upon the porch, as if I considered such vulgar matters beneath my notice.

Here, being soon joined by Tickle, and the day proving uncommonly fine, we set out on foot towards the city; and I was conducted by my friend to the door of my own lodgings.

CHAPTER IV.

IN WHICH SHEPPARD LEE HAS AN INTERVIEW WITH A LADY, WHO TELLS HIM A SECRET.

———

"In and mount," said Tickle: "I see Jem Puddle in the street yonder, and I have an idea I can borrow fifty dollars of him. I will drop round on you by-and-by."

So saying, Tickle started off and left me at the door of my lodgings. I had a sort of confused recollection of the place, though I had never seen it before in my life;—the dingy bricks and weather-stained marble, the rickety old iron railing on the steps, and the ugly, worn-out brass plate, with the "J. SNIGGLES" engraved thereon, rose on my memory like old acquaintances who had grown out of it. The house might have been a fashionable one in its day; nay, for the matter of that, it was not so humble in appearance but that a gentleman might have lived in it, if too poor to inhabit a better; and though out of the world, being in a street called Eighth, it was within hail of Chestnut: nevertheless, it was but a poor place compared with my late dwelling, *my* house, in Chestnut; the recollection of which, together with the reflection that I entered this only as a lodger, somewhat abated the transport of my joy. "Ah!" thought I, "what a pity, in giving up John H. Higginson's gout and wife, I had also to give up his house and money!" But the recollection of the two first-named possessions was fresh upon me, and I ceased to murmur.

I ascended the steps and rang the bell, somewhat faintly, I must acknowledge; for though I had my friend Tickle's assurance, and a confused consciousness of my own, that I was at the right place, there was a certain strangeness in it, naturally arising from my situation, that made me hesitate. The door, however, opened, and the reception that followed convinced me I was not intruding where I was not known.

The door was opened by a bouncing Irish wench, of some twenty-five years or thereabouts, with hair as yellow as a broom-whisk, and shoulders twice as broad as my own; besides which, she was not handsome; she had staring gray eyes, brick-coloured cheeks, a nose that looked up at her forehead, and a mouth not so ugly as spacious.

I was about to pass by this fair apparition with no further notice than a nod, which I made somewhat instinctively; but I was not fated to get off so easily. No sooner did she lay eyes upon me than she set up a squeak, "Oh,

- 95 -

hubbuboo! and is it _you_, Misther Dawkins, dear?" and threw her great beef-steak arms round my neck.

An embrace from a creature of her attractions I could have easily dispensed with; yet I might have been affected by her joy at seeing me return alive from the bottom of the river, it was so truly natural and exuberant, had she not been in a great hurry to qualify it. "Oh, murder, dear!" she cried, "and I'm glad; for they said, bad luck till'em, the vagabones! you was drownded, dear, and was after chating me out iv my money for the washin' and mindin'!"

"The washing and mending?" thought I. "Do I patronise such a tasty body as this? and do I owe her money?"

But while I muttered thus within, the girl, giving me another hug that I thought would have made my shoulders change place with one another, roared out, in continuation,—

"Och, throth, but the man must drown dape that chates Nora Magee of her own! Musha, hinny darlint, jist pit yer finger into yer pocket and pull me out the tin dollars and seventy cents that you owe me."

"Certainly, Nora," said I; "and Succuba let me go. But, ged now, Nora," I cried, for well I knew my pockets were as empty as the promises I intended to make her, and I was driven by a sort of instinct upon the proper course for pacifying the harpy,—a course, I suppose, that I,—that is, my prototype, the true Dawkins,—had often practised before;—I say, "Nora, don't talk of dollars and cents; for I intend to pay you in eagles and half-eagles some of these days, when my uncle comes; and besides, Nora, you jade you, I intend to give you a buss into the bargain, as, ged, I believe I will _now_."

And with that I returned the compliment she had paid me, took the great creature by the neck, and (yea, faith, and I presume I should have done the same thing with my tailor, if he could have been managed the same way) absolutely kissed her.

"Och! blessings on yer pritty face!" said she, looking pleased and disappointed together, but wiping her mouth as if to prepare for a second salute, "and that's the way you bamboozles me wid your uncles and your thricks upon a poor cratur's modesty! But, oh, Misther Dawkins, dear, ye'r lookin' sick and pokey; and so I'll not be after throubling you; and I hopes your uncle will be soon in Phillydelphy; for there's our ould Sniggles, the hungry ould nagur (that I should be saying so of the master o' the house, that gives me a dollar a week and a new bonnet at Christmas!) he's been rampin', and roarin', and swearin' like a Turk, my heavy hathred on him, he'll be havin' you up before the constables and squires for the dirty rint-money, the ould divil! that you owe him."

"The rent-money?" thought I; and I began to have a sort of feeling about me, I do not know what, but it was not agreeable. I clapped my hand into my pocket; there was a pocketbook there, but I had examined it before, and there was nothing in it. My mind began to misgive me a little; it was apparent the worthy I. D. Dawkins had not yielded me his body without leaving me some of his debts to pay: and as to what means of discharging them he might have bequeathed, I was yet in the dark.

I ascended to my rooms, of which I discovered I had a brace; but I was in some dudgeon to find them in the third story. "Very odd," said I to myself, "that I should be a fashionable man and a dandy, and live in a third story!" My instincts had gone nigh, as I climbed the stairs, to carry me into a chamber on the first floor; but, "Arrah, now, hinny," said Nora, "you'd be after forgetting you agreed to give up the best chambers till yer uncle comes to town—bad luck to him for keeping me so long out iv my tin dollars!"

"This uncle of mine," thought I, "will settle all pothers." But who he was, or what sort of claim I had upon him, I knew no more than the man in the moon. My associations acted but slowly and imperfectly, and when I strove to look back upon the past history of my new body, I felt like a man who has clapped upon his nose his grandmother's spectacles, through which he can behold objects indeed, but all so confused, distorted, and mystified, that they serve only to bewilder his vision. Thus I beheld, when I made the effort, a jumble of events and persons crowded together on my memory, but without being able to seize upon any one and examine it to my satisfaction. I had an uncle, it seemed, but I could not recall any thing like a recollection of having ever seen him. "But time," thought I, "will set these things right."

CHAPTER V.

AN INVENTORY OF A YOUNG GENTLEMAN'S EFFECTS, WITH SOME ACCOUNT OF MR. SNIGGLES, HIS LANDLORD.

My chambers were but meanly furnished, and this—But it needs not I should acquaint the reader with the divers proofs that rose every moment to convince me Mr. I. D. Dawkins, though a dandy, was not a rich one. Before I had rummaged an hour among his chattels, I discovered enough to set me into a cold shiver, and almost make me repent having taken possession of his body. I found lying upon his table no less than thirty-seven folded papers—the tribute doubtless of the two days of his absence—of which, eight were either billetsdoux or mere cards of invitation to ladies' parties, and twenty-nine were letters from tailors, shoemakers, &c., all of them requesting payment of money owed, and most of them as ferocious in spirit as they were original in style and grammar. In an old trunk, which I ransacked, as well as every chest of drawers and closet in the rooms (the keys were ready at hand in my pocket), I discovered a bushel or two of bills—I suppose there may have been a thousand of them, for they were of all dates—not one of which had a receipt to it.

But, to make amends for this evil, I found Mr. I. D. Dawkins's wardrobe in pretty good condition, except in the article of shirts; of which I discovered but six, and those none of the best. However, there were three dozen good dickeys, and a great abundance of loose collars and wristbands; with which, I perceived, I might do without shirts altogether.

But what gave me most pleasure, and indeed quite consoled me under the feelings of disappointment and doubt that had begun to rise, was a marvellous great quantity of love-letters, locks of hair, finger-rings, odd gloves, &c., that I found scattered about; each, as was apparent, the tribute or spoil of some admiring fair. "Aha!" said I, "I am a devil of a fellow among the girls: who can resist me?" The idea of being a favourite among the women, and the prospect I had of shooting conquests among them, right and left, were infinitely agreeable. "Ged and demmee," said I, "I will look about me now, and fix for life. I will pick out the finest creature I can find who has a fortune, and marry her; and then, I say, demm all tailors and other people. I will marry a wife, eged!"

It was doubly remarkable I should make such a resolution, having had but lately such a lesson of the joys of matrimony. But I found myself fast growing another man. I still retained a lively recollection of Mrs. Higginson, but fancy pictured an angel in the anticipated Mrs. Dawkins. Dim visions— which seemed to be made up as much of crude recollections as of half-formed anticipations—dim visions of lovely eyes and noses floated over my brain; I sank into a soft, elysium-like revery; when I suddenly heard a voice, somewhat tremulous and feeble, but rude as the screech of a strawberry-woman in spring, saying,

"Sir, I say, sir, Mr. Dawkins, I shall trouble you, I say, for the amount of that 'ere small account."

The accents were more horrible to my soul than the grating of a dentist's file upon the tenderest of grinders. I looked up from my feet, which I had been admiring, and beheld a visage somewhat iracund and savage, but so vulgar and plebeian in all its lineaments, that my fear was changed into contempt.

"And I say, sare! whoever you ah," said I, looking the fellow to the soul, "what do you want he-ah? who ah you?"

At these questions the man looked petrified; he opened his mouth till I thought his under jaw would drop off, and stared at me in dumb amazement. I had some hopes he was about to fall down in a fit. I am not naturally of a bloodthirsty turn; but I knew he was a dun, and such persons one always wishes the devil would snatch up. But he recovered his tongue, and, to do him justice, I must confess he used it with a spirit I did not look for in such a mean, shrivelled-up body as he had.

"Don't go for to insult me," said the Goth, gritting his teeth, and spluttering his words through them as through a watering-pot; "I'll let you know who I am. I'll have my money, or I'll have the worth on it out on you; for I won't be cheated no more for nothing. And as for what I'm doing here, I'll let you know as how I'm master in my own house; and, as Mrs. Sniggles says—"

"Sniggles!" said I, recollecting that the rascal was my landlord and creditor. I started up, and seizing the enraged little man by the hand, I begged his pardon.

"Really, my dear soul," said I, "I was in a brown study, and I didn't know you. Pray how d'ye do? how is Mrs. Sniggles? You must know I have hardly yet got over my unfortunate fall into the water. Really, sah, I was almost drowned, and I had the misfortune to lose my pocketbook."

"None on your gammon on me!" said Mr. Sniggles, looking as intrepid as ever; "for I don't believe none on it; and I don't believe you're no gentleman neither, or you wouldn't keep me out of my money. You see, Mr. Dawkins, do you see, you've had my rooms five months, and I ha'n't seen the colour on your money over once; it's all promise and no pay. And so, as I was saying, I won't be diddled no longer, or I'll see the end of it; for, as Mrs. Sniggles says, we can't afford to be diddled for nothing."

"Come, Sniggles," said I, "don't be in a passion; I'll pay you. What's the amount?"

"Seventeen weeks on the second story, seven dollars a week—monstrous cheap at that, considerin' there's breakfast in—one hundred and nineteen dollars—and taking off the ten dollars you paid me, as per account, one hundred and nine dollars; four weeks on the third story, at five dollars and a half (and good rooms too), twenty-two dollars; and adding the ten dollars I paid the shoe-maker, and the five dollars sixty cents I loaned you to pay the fine at the mayor's office, for smashing the lamp, makes jest a hundred and forty-one dollars sixty cents, no halves nor quarters, precise; and the sooner you shows me the money the better."

"A confounded long bill that, Sniggles," said I; "but I don't dispute it; and the moment my uncle comes to town—"

The mean, avaricious fellow had begun to look happy, as he conned over the hateful particulars of his account, which he held in his hand; but no sooner had the words "my uncle" left my lips, than he began to jump up and down, pulling his hair, gritting his teeth, and shaking his fists like a mad-man; and to my astonishment the contemptible fellow waxed profane, and actually cursed me and my uncle too. His oaths, as may be supposed, only made him appear more low-lived and vulgar than before; for cursing and swearing are the hardest things to do *genteelly* that I know: there are but few persons in the world who can produce an oath with any thing like elegance; it is the truest criterion of gentility, and in consequence I would recommend no person to attempt one who is not confident of his high breeding.

My landlord, Mr. Sniggles, fell to cursing and swearing, and insulted me very grossly; first, by affecting to believe that no such person as my uncle existed; secondly, by threatening to turn me out of his house; and thirdly, by assuring me he would have his account in an attorney's hands before I was an hour older. It was in vain I exhorted him to moderate his passion, and strove to wheedle him into a better humour; I had forgotten (or rather I did not yet know) the true secret of his character, which was cowardice, by addressing my arguments to which I might have readily brought him to reason. But, in truth, I was frightened myself; how I was to pay a bill of a hundred and forty-one dollars sixty cents was a thing only to be guessed at; and the prospect of taking up my lodgings in the debtors' apartments up Arch-street, was as vinegar and wormwood to my imagination.

The more I strove to sooth the wrath of Mr. Sniggles, the more ferocious he became; until at last he did nothing but dance round and round me, like a little dog barking at a big one that is tied to a post, crying out all the time, frantic with despair and fury, "Pay me what you owe me! pay this here bill here! pay me my money, or I'll have you in jail!" with other expressions equally foolish and insulting.

CHAPTER VI.

SHEPPARD LEE HEARS NEWS OF HIS UNCLE, AND MR. SNIGGLES IS BROUGHT TO HIS SENSES.

In the midst of my troubles, up comes my friend Tickle and pops into the room. He gave a stare at Sniggles, and next a grin; and then, just as I was looking to be laughed at, he made a spring and caught me round the neck, crying, with uncommon exultation and eagerness,—

"I congratulate you, Dawkins, you dog! and, mind, you must lend me five hundred dollars tomorrow!"

Before I could answer a word to this surprising address, he turned upon Sniggles, and, looking black as a thunder-cloud, cried,—

"Hah! Sniggles? What is the fellow doing here? dunning you for his money? The scoundrel! Hah! What!"

I thought he would have kicked the poor man out of the room, and so thought Sniggles also; for, though he exclaimed, "Touch me if you dare!" he ran to the door, where he looked vastly alarmed, and was able to muster only a single expression of resolution. "I asks my money," said he, "and dang me but I'll have it; for, as Mrs. Sniggles says, I'll not be diddled for nothing."

"Pay the rascal his dirty money, and then be done with him; leave his house, and patronise him no more," said Jack. Then turning to me, he made three skips into the air, clapped his hands, and running up to me and giving me a second embrace, cried,—

"Angels, horses, and women! hug me, kiss me, and lend me that five hundred dollars—your uncle has arrived!"

"Uncle! what uncle?" said I.

"Why your uncle Wiggins—your rich old uncle—your dad of an uncle—your bank and banker—your—But I say, Dawky, you'll lend me that five hundred, won't you? Saw him at the hotel—just arrived—asked anxiously for his nephew Dawkins;—bad look about the eyes—will die in a month; and then—*then*, my fellow! fourteen thousand a year, if it's fourteen hundred!"

"Fourteen thousand a year!" echoed I; the words were also muttered over by Sniggles. I caught the fellow's eye; he looked confounded and uneasy.

"If that's so," said he, "then I hope Mr. Dawkins will pay me my money, and not take no offence, for none wasn't intended."

"Pay you your money!" said Jack Tickle, stepping up to him in a rage; "no, you rapacious dun, he sha'n't pay you a cent. You shall sue him, and get judgment, and wait six months for your money."

"No, you rascallion!" said I, "I won't take that revenge of such a low fellow. I'll pay you your money, and be done with you. But, Jack, I say, demmee, let's be off; let's run down to my uncle Wiggins."

"Wiggins!" said my landlord; "why, you always said his name was Wilkins!"

"And so it is," said Tickle; "Wiggins P. Wilkins, the rich and well-known Wiggins P. Wilkins. But what do you want here? Have you had your answer? What do you mean by intruding here? You'll get your money; and so, if you please, do Mr. Dawkins and me the favour to walk down stairs, or—"

"Well," said my amiable creditor, whose fury was quite overcome by Tickle's violence, and his report of my uncle's arrival, "I always said Mr. Dawkins was a gentleman, and would pay me one day or another; and one day's just as good as another; and so I hopes he'll take no offence. But as for you, and the likes of you, Mr. Tickle," said the little man, endeavouring to assume courage, "I don't like to be abused in my own house; but, howsomever, as you're Mr. Dawkins's friend, I'll say no more about it."

And with that my gentleman walked down stairs.

"Let us go!" said I. "Let us run—let us fly!"

"Where?" said Tickle.

"Why, to my uncle. Where is he?"

"Where!" cried Tickle, bursting into a roar of laughter. "Are you as big a fool as Sniggles? You didn't believe me! Ah, lud! is there nobody witty but myself?"

"And my uncle a'n't come, then?" said I. "What made you say so?"

"To rid you of a dun, my fellow," said Jack. "I saw the rascal had worked himself into a phrensy, and that you were at your wit's end. I had pity on your distresses, and so ran in with a huge lie, as irresistible as a broadsword, to the rescue. Victory and Jo Pæan! I have routed the enemy, and you are no longer in fear. Keep up the fire, and you are easy for a week."

"But my uncle really intends to leave me that fourteen thousand a year?" said I.

"Has he got it?" said Jack, giving me a comical stare.

"Jack," said I, after pausing a little, "I want to ask you a favour."

"Have but twenty-five in the world," said Tickle, pulling out his pocketbook; "but you shall have ten."

"It isn't that," said I; "I want you to tell me my history."

"Your history!" said Tickle, staring at me in surprise.

CHAPTER VII.

IN WHICH SHEPPARD LEE IS TOLD HIS HISTORY.

An idea had suddenly seized me; and I must say, that up to this time, it was the most brilliant one that ever entered my mind. My ignorance of Mr. I. D. Dawkins's affairs was still highly inconvenient and oppressive, and I was determined, with my friend's assistance, to remove it.

"Tickle," said I, "I really believe the doctor has only half resuscitated me; my body is pretty well, but my mind is only so-so. Would you believe it, my memory is quite gone?"

"As to your debts, certainly," said Jack; "so is mine."

"Ged," said I, "'tis gone altogether. Really, it seems to me as if I had only begun existence this morning; my recollection of all events (and even persons known) anterior to my sop in the river, is so imperfect, you can't conceive. Would you believe it, I really didn't know that rogue Sniggles, and had to ask him his name! The ladies, too, Jack—Miss Smith, Miss Small, and the rest that you were talking about—who the deuse are they? I have heard much talk of my uncle, too. *Have* I an uncle? and if so, who and what is he? for I swear, 'pon honour, Jack, I know no more than the man in the moon. In a word, Jack, demmee, I am in my second childhood, and you must help me out of it. Give me, therefore, my history, my whole history, and tell me all about me; for may I be dunned to death if I rightly know who I am!"

"You don't?" said Jack; "well, that's funny; but I have heard of such things before. Is a dip in cold water, then, so hard on the memory? I say, Dawky, my fellow, couldn't we contrive some way to dip our creditors? But, eged now, Dawky, you a'n't serious?"

"I am," said I; "and I beg you'll give me an idea who I am, and all other things appertaining."

"Oh!" said Tickle, who seemed vastly diverted by my embarrassment, "that is soon done. You are a dandy of pure blood, and poor as a church mouse, but not yet out of favour. Your father, who was a dandy before you, and in prime esteem, having bought his way into notice with two or three cargoes of indigo and young hyson (for he was an India merchant), properly laid out in elegant entertainments, gave up trade to live a gentleman, and died one; leaving you, an elegant fellow and ignoramus, as a gentleman's son should be, to spend his leavings. This you have done, Dawky, and most gloriously. For five years, none of us, the sons of nabobocracy, could compare with you in dash, flash, and splash. But even Phaeton fell! Horses galloped away, buggies and curricles rolled into the gutter, and tailors looked alarmed—stocks flew out at the window, bricks and mortar took to themselves wings, and your stockings began to want darning. Then said Dawkins, 'I will marry a wife,' and he looked loving at Periwinkle's fair daughter; and Periwinkle's fair daughter looked loving at Dawkins; and Dawkins calling counsel of his friend, John Tickle, of Ticklesbury Manor, beheld and lo! Periwinkle's fair daughter's father's fine estate was fenced round with rows of mortgages, as thick and thorny as prickly-pears. Whereupon the inconstant swain, forgetting his vows, ran to the elegant Miss Small, who smiled on him, and married another; and the loss of this adorable fair, fortune and all, together with an uncommon fit of dunning, so affected my friend's spirits, that he threw himself into the Schuylkill, whence he was fished by a fellow called What-d'-ye-call-it, a brewer."

"Well," said I; "but do you mean to say I have squandered all my property?"

"Every sous," said my friend; "it is just six weeks since you spent the last dollar of the last term of your annuity."

"What annuity?" said I.

"Why, the five years' annuity you bought of old Goldfist. Is it possible you don't recollect *him*? Don't you remember the row of negro-houses you owned down in Southwark?"

"I don't," said I.

"A piece of arrant cheating! sheer swindling!" said Tickle; "but when did old Skinner ever make an honest bargain? The houses and lot of ground worth two thousand, as they stood; but title good and indefeisible, and capable of being made worth twenty thousand: I remember you offered 'em to old Goldfist for seven. What said the old hunks? 'Give me immediate possession, and thereupon you shall have a bonus of a thousand on the nail, together with the same sum yearly for five years, provided you live so long—if not, then as long as you live.' Snapped like a gudgeon, and was bit; and on the fifth year—beginning of August last, had the last integer of payment, with comfort of seeing a property you had sold for six thousand, yielding its possessor just that much a year."

"The geds!" said I; "has old Goldfist six thousand a year?"

"Say sixty," replied Jack.

"Tickle," said I, "the old curmudgeon has a daughter: I'll marry her."

"No you won't," said my friend, shaking his head mournfully: "old Goldfist is too well acquainted with your affairs; and unless you have his consent, what will you get by her?"

"Tickle," said I, "I must marry somebody, or be ruined. But stay, there's my uncle; now, my dear fellow, who is he?"

"Faith," said Tickle, "I don't know; always supposed he belonged to the Apocrypha, and was used to argue duns into good manners: nobody sues a young fellow that has good expectations from a rich uncle. But, now I think of it, I believe you did once tell me you had an uncle—some vagabond trading fellow or other—in the west; but I never heard you say you expected any thing of him. I thought you called him Wiggins; but Sniggles says Wilkins. All's one, however; for I remember you said he had brats of his own."

I began to feel uncomfortable; and, upon questioning my friend further, I discovered that my situation was far from being agreeable. I had a horrible quantity of debts on my shoulders, and no fund to discharge them; and, what was worse, I found that my means of subsistence were not only precarious, but I had good reason to fear they were any thing but reputable. My dear friend John Tickle, though a gentleman and dandy, it was plain, was a personage who lived by his wits; and I began to see that Mr. I. D. Dawkins was another. From Tickle's expressions, I perceived that our chief dependance lay in the noble trade of pigeon-hunting. As this is a word some of my readers may be too unsophisticated to understand, I will explain it, and in very few words. As there are in the world young fellows of plebeian origin but full pockets, who are ambitious to figure in elegant society, so there are also in elegant society sundry youths of better fame than fortune, who are willing to patronise them, provided any thing can be made by their condescension; in which case, the happy Phaeton is taught to spend his money in ways most advantageous to his patrons, though by no means to his own profit. Such a young gentleman is then called a pigeon, and is allowed to flutter in the sunbeams, while his eagle-clawed friends are helping themselves to his feathers; the last of which being abstracted, he is commonly called a fine fellow, and kicked out of their company. I cannot pretend to say what degree of relish my prototype, the true I. D. Dawkins, may have had for such a mode of existence; but I must aver in my own defence, that I had, throughout the whole adventure, while in his body, so much of Sheppard Lee's original sense of honour and honesty hanging about me, that I was more than once shocked at the meanness and depravity of such a course of life; and when I first understood the thing from Tickle, I was so ashamed of myself, that had I lighted upon the body of any decent man at the moment, I do verily believe I should have done my best to get into it, and so put an end to Mr. I. D. Dawkins altogether.

But men's bodies are not like the dry-goods dealers' boxes in Market-street, to be stumbled into at any moment.

It was some comfort to me to find that our practice in this particular was so little known, that both Tickle and myself—but myself more especially— were considered in the main very excellent, exemplary young men, as far as dandies could be, and were still allowed to mingle in elegant society.

As for Tickle, indeed, I soon discovered he was in but doubtful odour with the ladies, at least with their mammas; for he had been for some years living on his wits: but I, on the contrary, being pretty universally regarded as the heir-expectant of a rich uncle, and being besides a prettier fellow, was received with general favour and approbation.

Having obtained from Tickle as much of my (or Mr. I. D. Dawkins's) history as was necessary, I gave my worthy friend to understand I should need his advice and assistance in returning into society; "for," said I, and very truly too, "I really sha'n't know anybody, and shall feel very awkward. Here," I added, "are two invitations for this very evening—one from Mrs. Pickup, and the other from the Misses Oldstyle. Now who is Mrs. Pickup? and who are the Oldstyles? and where the mischief do they live?"

"It is very odd you should forget so much," said Tickle; and then proceeded to give me the information I wanted, promising also to go with me to both places himself, and prompt me through all difficulties.

CHAPTER VIII.

A CONVERSATION WITH A TAILOR. SHEPPARD LEE FINDS HIMSELF IN A SITUATION TRULY APPALLING.

Having thus got upon the subject of the ladies, we—that is, Tickle and myself—fell into a highly agreeable conversation, in the course of which I lost sight of all my fears and anxieties, until they were suddenly recalled by the entrance—and a very unceremonious one it was—of a tall fellow with hinge knees and crow-bar elbows, fashionably dressed, but whom there was no mistaking for aught but a vulgarian. I knew his errand before he spoke; and so did Tickle, who instantly cried out,

"Snip the tailor, eged! and another paroxysm of dunning!"

"Servant, Mr. Dawkins,—servant, Mr. Tickle," said the gentleman, giving each of us a scrape; "hope no intrusion and no offence; wouldn't go to controvert gentlemen on no account. But, talking of accounts, Mr. Dawkins, hope you'll excuse me; wouldn't dun a gentleman for the world, but have a cussed note in bank for cloth, and must make up the sum by to-morrow; and so, if it's convenient, Mr. Dawkins, shall be obliged for the amount of bill."

"My uncle," said I—

"Can't go that no more," said the tailor; "can't go that no more, begging pardon. Bill outstanding nineteen months and over; wouldn't mind letting it run the year out, but for the cussed pressure on the money-market: no money to be had nowhere."

"Right," said Jack; "and what makes you suppose you will get it here? Now, Snip, my dear fellow, make yourself short. 'Tis not convenient just now for my friend Dawkins to pay you."

"Must take up that note," said Mr. Snip; "can't think of waiting no longer."

The rascal spoke resolutely, though more cowardly-looking than Sniggles: but who could withstand the rage and indignation of my friend Tickle?

"Away, you ungrateful loon!" said he; "is that the way you serve the man that made you? Who would have employed you, you botch, if Dawkins had not taken you up and made you fashionable?"

"Ay, demmee, Snip," said I, taking my cue from Tickle, "I say, wasn't I the making of you? and do you come dunning me? Didn't I recommend you into notice and business? didn't I send my friends to you?"

"Can't deny," said the tailor, "won't controvert; but must say, can't always get my money of Mr. Dawkins's friends; but don't mean no offence. Wouldn't think of pressing Mr. Dawkins; always said he was my friend; wouldn't mind holding back, if Mr. Dawkins would send me good pay-customers."

"Well," said I, thinking the man was modest in his desires, "I will: you shall have three Johnny Raws before the week is out, and you may charge them double."

"Very much obliged, and won't controvert," said Mr. Snip, humbly; "but can't take no more promises."

"And you really insist upon having your money?" said Tickle.

"Ay!" said I, re-echoing his indignation, and putting on a dignity that even awed myself, "you are determined to have your money, and to lose your business? Tickle, hand me back that five hundred I lent you, or enough of it to pay the rascallion—shall have it again as soon as I can run down and see my uncle Wilkins. I say, Tickle, hand me the money, and let me pay the ungrateful rascal off."

"If I do," said Jack, "demmee! Encourage dunning? Never!"

"He shall have his money," said I. "Here, you Snip, you man, you have broken your own neck; come back here to-morrow at half past twelve, with a receipt in full, take your money, and never look to make a gentleman's coat again. Come, Tickle, it is time I was with my uncle; you shall go along and dine with him. A fine old cock, I assure you!"

I surveyed the tailor; my dignity, and the sound of my uncle's name, had subdued him. He slipped his bill into his pocket, and looked penitent.

"Won't controvert a gentleman on no occasion," he said. "Always said Mr. Dawkins was my friend; and as for Mr. Dawkins's uncle—"

"Yes!" said Jack, "yes! you said you did not believe in any such person! did not believe there was such a person!"

"Can't controvert no gentleman," said the tailor, looking as if he had been rubbed down with his own goose; "but never said no such thing, Mr. Tickle. Always believed in Mr. Dawkins's uncle, but only thought perhaps he wouldn't pay—that is, wasn't certain, and didn't mean no offence; and so if Mr. Dawkins will say a word for me now and then to gentlemen that wants coats, I'll leave it to his convenience; hoping he will excuse my coming up stairs without asking, not having found no servant, and not supposing he would take no offence, and—"

And so the rascallion was going on, heaping apology on apology, and about to depart in contrition for his offence; when, as my evil genius would have it, in popped Mr. Sniggles, foaming with wrath, and looking daggers and conflagration.

"Trouble you for the amount of that 'ere small account," said the fellow; "don't believe in no more uncles; won't be diddled no longer for nothing; all diddle about uncle—just as Mrs. Sniggles says—no more uncle than she has!"

"What do you mean?" said Jack Tickle; but his indignation no longer daunted the dun, who cried out, with uncommon emphasis and effect,—

"Had my doubts about the matter, and told Mrs. Sniggles, said I, 'Mr. Dawkins's uncle has come;' says Mrs. Sniggles, 'Run down to the tavern and see; for no sitch thing a'n't certain till we knows it.' And so I runs down to the Mansion House, and Mr. Wilkins wasn't there; and then I runs to the United States, hoping it was a mistake, and Mr. Wilkins wasn't there; and then I runs to this place and that place, and Mr. Wilkins wasn't there; and, as Mrs. Sniggles said, Mr. Wilkins wasn't nowhere, but 'twas all diddle, and throwing dust in my eyes. And so, as for this here account, one hundred and forty-one dollars sixty—"

"Don't controvert no one," said Mr. Snip, who had listened all agape to the outpourings of the other, and now turned his battery upon me again, "but can't think of keeping the account open no longer; don't want to be hard upon any gentleman, but must have my money."

"One hundred and forty-one dollars sixty cents," said Sniggles.

"Two hundred and thirty-seven," said Snip.

But why should I detail the particulars of that eventful hour? Even Tickle's courage sank before the fire of the enraged assailants; and as for mine, had it been fortified by a heart of steel and ribs of brass, it must have yielded to the horrors that followed. Duns follow the same laws as flies and carrion-crows; no sooner does one swoop at a victim, than down drop a thousand others to share the feast. Scarce had my landlord and the tailor begun the assault, when there sneaked into the room a consumptive-looking fellow, smelling strongly of leather and rosin, who displayed a greasy scrap of paper, and added his pipe to the others. Then came another, with inky hands, a black spot on his nose, and a new hat under his arm; then another, and another, and another; until I believe there were fourteen different souls in the room (or rather *bodies*, for I don't think they had one soul among them), all of them armed with long bills, all clamorous for their money, and all (each being encouraged by the example of the others) as noisy, mad, and ferocious as any mob of free and independent republicans I ever laid eyes on. Such a siege of dunning was perhaps never endured, except by a poor dandy. They dunned and they dinned, they poked out their ugly bills, and they gave loose to their inhuman tongues,—in a word, they conducted in such a manner that I was more than once inclined to jump out the window, being driven to complete desperation.

In the midst of all, and when I saw no escape whatever from my persecutions, they were brought to a close by a most unexpected incident. The door flew open, and in rushed—not a fifteenth tormentor, as I expected—but an angel of light in the person of Nora Magee, who screamed out at the top of her voice,—

"Och, hinny darlint, your uncle, Misther Wiggins, has come! and in a beautiful carriage! and he looks as if he could pay your ditts twice over! Sure, now, and ye'll ax him for my tin dollars?"

CHAPTER IX.

THE AUTHOR RECEIVES A VISIT FROM HIS UNCLE, SAMUEL WILKINS, ESQ., AND IS RELIEVED FROM HIS TORMENTORS.

Let the reader judge of the effect of such an announcement upon my tormentors and myself. I had an uncle, then, and he had arrived—nay, he had paid me a visit, and was in the house; I could hear him stumping up the stairs! My debtors were struck dumb, and so was I; and at that moment of confusion he stepped into the room. I looked at the gentleman, and, upon my soul, I was somewhat disappointed. His appearance was scarce genteel enough for *my* uncle; he looked like a country squire of low degree, who might pass for a man of quality better in an unsophisticated village of the backwoods than anywhere else; and he had an atrocious white fur hat, with a big brim all puckered and twisted like the outer casing of a cabbage. There was a vulgar vivacity and good-nature about his visage, an air of presumption and familiarity in his motions, and his nose turned up. On the whole, I did not like his appearance, and my first impulse was to give him a look of contempt; but I recollected he was my uncle, and had come in a carriage; and seeing him stand staring about in great astonishment, as not knowing what to make of such a rout of ragamuffins as I had about me, nor how to distinguish his nephew among them, I stepped up to him, and taking him by the hand, said,—

"My dear saw, ah! looking for me? What! my uncle Wiggins?"

"*Wiggins!*" said he; "ods bobs, don't you know the name of your own uncle Wilkins?"

"Wiggins?" said I; "ged, 'twas a mere slip of the tongue."

"Ods bobs!" said he, "and is this you, Ikey, my boy? The very picture of your aunt, poor Mrs. Wilkins! but, ods bless her, she's dead. Ha'n't seen you since you was a baby; do declare, you're as big as Sammy. Come to live in your town, Ikey, my dear; tired of living among the clodhoppers; have plenty of money, and mean to be a gentleman now. Glad to see you, Ikey; but I say, Ikey, who is all these here people? Always heard you was a great gentleman; but don't much like your acquaintance, Ikey."

This was pronounced in an under voice, much to my satisfaction; for the liberty the old gentleman took with my name was not grateful to my feelings. *Ikey*, indeed! None but a vulgarian would have made so free with me.

But he was my uncle, he said he was rich, and I perceived he might be made serviceable.

I shook him by the hand a dozen times over, swore "I was so glad to see him he could not conceive;" assured him—in his ear—the fellows he saw were ambitious cobblers and stitchers, who had come to beg my favour and recommendation to the fashionable circles, for my countenance was a fortune, and the rascals *would* persecute me; declared my friend Tickle, who stood enjoying the scene from a corner, was a young blood and intimate, who had just lent me a thousand dollars to pay a poor fellow who was in distress; and concluded by assuring him, that as I did not like being obliged to a man *not* a near kinsman, I would hand the sum back again, and borrow it of *him* if he had brought so much to town with him.

The warm welcome with which I began my speech greatly delighted my uncle's heart, as I saw; my apology for the appearance of the duns, it was evident, caused him to look upon me as a young fellow of great importance and distinction; the reference to the young blood who had just lent me a thousand dollars, confirmed his opinion of my lofty stand among the rich and fashionable; and to all these members of my discourse he hearkened with respect and satisfaction; but when I arrived at my climax, and professed a readiness to borrow that sum of himself, I thought his eyes would drop out of his head, they stared out so far. In a word, I perceived that, let him be as rich as he might, he was not the man to lend me money; for which reason I despised the relationship more than ever, and resolved to disown it as soon as my convenience would permit. But it was proper to make it useful at the present moment.

I turned round upon my duns, who were yet in confusion. "Gentlemen," said I, giving them a bow of dismission, "I will remember your claims; you may depend upon me; but at present, as you see, I must attend to those of my excellent uncle. You understand me, ehem."

"Ehem," said they all; and I thought they would have all turned somersets, so profound were their congees, as, one by one, they sneaked out of the room. The only ones who hesitated were my landlord, Nora Magee, and Snip the tailor. The first was probably overcome by a sense of having dunned me too hard, and despair of forgiveness; on which supposition I gave him a frown, and waved my hand, and he retired. As for Nora, she perhaps loitered to feast her eyes with the spectacle of the rich man, from whose pockets were to be drawn her ten dollars; but I gave her a wink (a very vulgar way of conveying a hint, I confess—but one can't be genteel with one's creditors), and she rolled smiling away. What kept the tailor I could not say; till, having given him divers significant looks and gestures, he began to drawl out, "Can't controvert no gentleman, but—" when I stepped up to him, took him by the arm, and led him from the apartment.

"What, you dog," said I, in a familiar, affectionate sort of way, as soon as I had him out of my uncle's hearing, "do you want to raise a hubbub, and put the old fellow in a passion? Come, you rogue, your fortune's made:—seven grown sons—seven broadcloth suits a year (extravagant dogs they!)—shall have them all, you shall, upon my honour: can twist the young apes round my finger, and you shall have'em. Seven times seven is forty-nine, seven fifties is three thousand and odd; 'ged and demmee, you'll make a fortune out of them!"

With that I pushed the giggling cormorant down stairs, and ran back to my uncle.

CHAPTER X.

SOME ACCOUNT OF SHEPPARD LEE'S COUNTRY KINSMEN.

"Adieu!" said Tickle, giving me a nod, as much as to say, "Make the most of the old gentleman;" he then imitated the duns, and left me; a circumstance for which I was not sorry, for I was somewhat ashamed of my uncle.

"Fine-looking young fellow that," said Mr. Wilkins; "must be a rich dog to lend you a thousand dollars. But I say, Ikey—"

"Uncle Wiggins—that is, Wilkins," said I, "I beg you won't call me by any such vulgar nickname as Ikey. I can't abide nicknames; they are horrid plebeian."

"Ods bobs," said my uncle, "I call my son Sammy, Sammy and Sam too—"

"What," said I, "have you a son?"

"Ods bobs!" said he; "why, didn't you know? I say, nevvy, your dad and me was never good friends; proud as a turkey-cock—thought me a democrat and no great shakes, but I snapped up his sister though; and so there was never no love lost between us: never knew much about one another, especially him. But I say, nevvy, ods bobs, don't be a fool, and despise like your dad; could buy him six times over if he was alive, and don't suppose you're much richer; and don't value you a new pin. Don't pretend you didn't know I had a son; might as well say you didn't know I had a daughter."

The old gentleman looked somewhat incensed: I hastened to pacify him, by assuring him I had had a violent fit of sickness and lost my memory. I then drew from him without difficulty as much of his history and affairs as I cared to know.

Although of a vulgar stock, his face had, somehow or other, captivated the fancy of my father's sister, who very ungenteelly ran off with him, and accompanied him to some interior village of the state, where the happy swain sold tapes and sugar, that being his profession. Here, although discountenanced and despised by his wife's family, he gradually amassed wealth, and in course of time mightily increased it, by laying his hands on those four great staples of the Susquehanna, iron, lumber, coal, and whiskey. In fine, having scraped together enough for his purpose, he yielded to a design which his wife had first put into his plebeian head, and which his children, as they grew up, took care to stimulate into action: this was, to exchange his village for the metropolis, his musty warehouses for elegant saloons, and live, during the remainder of his life, a nabob and gentleman; and in this design, as I discovered, he expected to derive no little aid from my humble self, who, being, as he said, a gentleman cut and dried, and knowing to all such matters, could give him a hint or two about high life, and help his children, the hopeful Sammy and the interesting Pattie (for such were their horrid names), into good society. The first step of his design he had already taken, having wound up his business and got him to Philadelphia, with his brats, both of whom were now safely lodged in a hotel, burning to make the acquaintance of their fashionable cousin, my distinguished self; and to these worthy kinsfolk he proposed to carry me forthwith.

I debated the matter in my mind: Should I acknowledge the claims of a brace of rustics with two such names? Sammy Wilkins! Pattie Wilkins! I felt that an old coat or a patched shoe could not more endanger my reputation, than two cousins named Sammy and Pattie. But the old man was rich, and some good might arise from my condescension. I agreed to go with him, and asked him at what hotel he had put up.

"Oh," said he, "at a mighty fine place—the What-d'-ye-call-it, in Market-street."

"In Market-street!" said I, and I thought his nose looked more democratic than ever. "Horrible! vulgar beyond expression! How came you to stop in such a low place? Can't expect any decent man to go nigh you. Must carry you to Head's without a moment's delay, or you'll be ruined for ever."

"Ods bobs," said my uncle, "it's a very good tavern, with eating and drinking for a king; but if it's not fashionable, sha'n't stay there no longer; shall go with us, nevvy, and show us the way to What-d'-ye-call-it's. The hack will just hold four."

I go to a tavern in Market-street? The idea was offensive; and ride thither, and afterward, my three country kinsfolk with me, to Head's, in a hackney-coach! The Market-street tavern and the hackney-coach finished my uncle Wilkins. I suddenly recollected a highly important engagement, which would deprive me of the pleasure of going round with my excellent uncle that moment, to make the acquaintance of my worthy cousins; nay, I feared it would occupy me all that evening, being an engagement of a very peculiar nature. I would see them the next day, when they were safely lodged at Head's, whither I recommended Mr. Wilkins to proceed, bag and baggage, instanter. My uncle accepted my excuses, and agreed to follow my advice, with a ready docility that might have pleased me, seeing that it showed the respect in which he held me; but I perceived in it nothing more than a willingness to be put into leading-strings, arising from his consciousness of inferiority.

I got rid of him, and resolved I would consider the pros and cons before compromising my reputation by any public acknowledgment of relationship.

Then, being vastly tired by the varied business of the day, I threw myself on my bed, where I slept during the remainder of the day very soundly and agreeably.

CHAPTER XI.

CONTAINING A MORSEL OF METAPHYSICS, WITH A SHORT ACCOUNT OF THE AUTHOR'S EXPERIENCE IN GOOD SOCIETY.

I was roused about nine o'clock in the evening by Tickle, who came, according to promise, to squire me to Mrs. Pickup's and the Misses Oldstyle's; and dressing myself in Mr. Dawkin's best, I accompanied him forthwith to the mansion of the former.

It was yet summer, and the season of gayety was therefore afar off. All genteel people were, or were supposed to be, out of town, according to the rule which, at this season, drives the gentry of London to their country-seats. The few of Philadelphia who could imitate the lords and ladies in this particular, were now catching agues on the Schuylkill; while the mass, consisting of those whose revenues did not allow any rustication on their own lands, were killing sand-flies on the seashore, or gnawing tough beef and grumbling over bad butter at some fashionable watering-place in the interior. There were some, however, as there always are, who considered themselves genteel, and who stayed at home, either because they were tired of agues, sand-flies, tough beef, and bad butter, as they freely professed; because they really believed they were better off at home; or because they were, like me and my friend Tickle, not rich enough to squander their money on vanities, and so stayed at home from necessity.

Of such persons one can always, even in summer-time, assemble enough to make a party of some kind or other, where the contented guests can be uncommonly sociable, eat ices, and pity their friends, who may be at the moment roasting in a ball-room at Saratoga.

It was undoubtedly a great misfortune that I should make my first introduction to good society at a time when it was to be seen only in its minimum of splendour; whereby I lost the opportunity of being dazzled to the same degree in which I found myself capable of dazzling others. Nevertheless, I was vastly captivated by what I saw, and for the few brief weeks that my destiny permitted me to live among the refined and exclusive, I considered myself an uncommonly happy individual.

The reception I met at Mrs. Pickup's convinced me that, in entering Mr. Dawkins's body, I had done the wisest thing in the world; for, however much it endangered me with the tailors, it proved the best recommendation to the ladies. I found myself ushered into a suite of apartments magnificently furnished and lighted, and not so over crowded (for the season was taken into consideration) but that the moschetoes had room to exercise their talents. I thought I should be devoured by Mrs. Pickup, she was so amazingly glad to see me; but I perceived, by a sort of instinct I had acquired along with Dawkins's body, that there was something plebeian about her, although a very fine woman as far as appearances went; and, indeed, Tickle assured me she was a mere *parvenue*, or upstart, whom everybody despised, and whom no one would come nigh, were it not for her wealth, and the resolution she avowed to give six different balls of the most splendid character in the course of the season. She had a daughter, who was very handsome, and a decided speculation; but I did not think much of her, especially as I found she was already engaged to be married.

I found here that I knew everybody, or, what was the same thing, that everybody knew me; and, with Tickle's help, I soon found myself as much at home with Mr. I. D. Dawkins's fair acquaintances as if I had known them all my life. It was still, as it had been before, a virtue and peculiarity of my recollections, that they were always roused by a few words of conversation with any one known to my prototype; from which I infer, that the associations of the mind, as well as many of its other qualities, are more dependant upon causes in the body than metaphysicians are disposed to allow.

This dependance it has been my fate to know and feel more extensively, perhaps, than any other man that ever lived. The spirit of Sheppard Lee was widely different from those of John H. Higginson and I. D. Dawkins, as, I think, the reader must have already seen; and yet, no sooner had it entered the bodies of these two individuals, than the distinction was almost altogether lost. Certain it is, that in stepping into each, I found myself invested with new feelings, passions, and propensities— as it were, with a new mind—and retaining so little of my original character, that I was perhaps only a little better able to judge and reason on the actions performed in my new body, without being able to avoid them, even when sensible of their absurdity.

I do verily believe that much of the evil and good of man's nature arises from causes and influences purely physical; that valour and ambition are as often caused by a bad stomach as ill-humour by bad teeth; that Socrates, in Bonaparte's body, could scarce have been Socrates, although the combination might have produced a Timoleon or Washington; and, finally, that those sages who labour to improve the moral nature of their species, will effect their purpose only when they have physically improved the stock. Strong minds may be indeed operated upon without regard to bodily bias, and rendered independent of it; but ordinary spirits lie in their bodies like water in sponges, diffused through every part, affected by the part's affections, changed with its changes, and so intimately united with the fleshly matrix, that the mere cutting off of a leg, as I believe, will, in some cases, leave the spirit limping for life.

But, as I said before, I am not writing a dissertation on metaphysics, nor on morals either; and as my adventures will suggest such reflections to all who care to indulge them, I will omit them for the present, and hasten on with my story.

And here the reader may expect of me a description of those scenes and persons in fashionable life to which and whom I was now introduced; and if I valued the reader's approbation at a higher price than my own conscience and reputation, I should undoubtedly gratify him, by putting my imagination in requisition, and painting at once some dozen or two of such fanciful pictures as are found in novels of fashionable life, though never, I opine, in fashionable life itself. In such I should have occasion to represent gentlemen more elegant and witty, and ladies more charming and ethereal, than are to be found in any of the ordinary circles of society; but, as I am writing truth and not fiction, and represent things as I found, not as I imagined them, I declare that the ladies and gentlemen of the exclusive circles to which I was admitted, were very much like the ladies and gentlemen of other circles —that is, as elegant and witty as they could be, and as charming and celestial as it pleased Heaven:—and that, after due exercise of judgment and memory, I cannot, in the adventures of three whole weeks in such society, remember a single person or thing worth describing. For which reason I will pass on to more important matters.

———————————————

CHAPTER XII.

SHEPPARD LEE MAKES THE ACQUAINTANCE OF HIS COUSIN, MISS PATTIE WILKINS.

Although I now look upon those three weeks of my life as three weeks of existence out of which I cheated myself, I was nevertheless so greatly delighted at first by the way in which I spent them, that I had almost forgotten my uncle Wilkins; and when I did think of him, it was only with renewed contempt and indifference. Finding, however, that the old fellow had called upon me three or four times during my absence from my lodgings, on as many different days, and remembering what he had said of his riches, it occurred to me that I might as well pay him a visit, were it only to satisfy Mr. Sniggles and Nora Magee, both of whom manifested great uneasiness at my undutiful conduct. It occurred to me, moreover, that although my uncle Wilkins was not a lending man, my cousin Sammy might be; and as I had now existed four different days without a single sixpence in my pocket, and began to be heartily ashamed of such a state of things, I thought it would be as well to pay the rustics a visit; and putting on a new coat which Snip had just sent me, to seal our reconciliation and secure my seven extravagant cousins, I started off forthwith.

As my evil luck would have it, I found the old gentleman on the point of setting out to pay me a fifth visit, and I had the satisfaction, just as I placed my foot on the porch of the hotel, in full view of some half a dozen respectable-looking people who were congregated there, to receive an embrace from Mr. Samuel Wilkins, with the old white fur hat, accompanied by a vocal salutation of, "Oho! Ikey, my boy, and so you *have* come, have you? Ods bobs, but I began to think you was ashamed of your relations.!"

"Not I," said I; "I am never ashamed of my relations." And I looked around me with dignity, so that all present might perceive I was condescending. I supposed I should find some of the spectators giggling, but was agreeably surprised when I beheld among them nothing but grave looks of respect. Indeed, two or three old gentlemen that I knew by sight, and who were what you call "stanch citizens"—that is, rich old fellows, not very genteel, but highly respected—made me low bows; and I heard one of them, as I passed with my uncle into the hotel, whisper to another, "It is the rich old rascal's nephew; quite a promising young man."

I began to feel a greater esteem for my uncle, for I saw that others respected him. Everybody seemed to know him and make way for him;

seeing which, I grew more condescending than ever, and instantly began to apologize for my seeming neglect, by pleading that I had been engaged night and day in preparing the way for the admission of him and my cousins, Sammy and Pattie, into good society.

"You want a house in a fashionable quarter," said I—

"Ods bobs," said he, "yes; and I've been looking all over town, from the glass-works down to the navy-yard, and seen a power of them."

"I flatter myself I can suit you," said I, "and better than you can yourself. Besides," said I, "I have been looking for carriages and horses."

"Why," said my uncle, "it's expensive keeping horses in a city; and I was against it; but there's Pattie says we can't do without 'em."

"Exactly so," said I: "you must live like a gentleman, or there's no getting or keeping in society. And, besides, I have been stirring up the beaux and belles to come and see my cousin, the fair—I say, uncle, eged, has she no other name than Pattie?"

"Yes," said my uncle Wilkins, "there's Abby,—that's Abigail—Martha Abigail Wilkins; called her after her grandmother and aunt, and hoped aunt Abby would leave her something; but she didn't."

Martha Abigail Wilkins! Worse and worse; I despaired of doing any thing, if I even wished it, for a creature with such a name.

But what I had done—that is, what I *said* I had done (for I had done nothing), had produced a great effect on my uncle, and put him into such a good-humour with me, that he seized me by the hand, swore I was the right sort of a dog after all, and, reaching the door of his private parlour, where the fair Martha Abigail was sitting, he kicked it open, crying aloud,

"Here, Pattie, you puss, here's your cousin Ikey, the dandy—as fine a whole-hog fellow as ever you saw—ods bobs, give 'm a buss."

I looked upon the unsophisticated rustic who was called upon to manifest her breeding in such an agricultural style; and, upon my soul, I was quite surprised to find in her, the aforesaid Pattie Abigail, one of the nicest little creatures I had ever laid eyes on, of a most genteel figure, tolerably well dressed, considering she had been brought up in the country, and with a sweet, prudish face, that was quite agreeable to look on.

She smiled and she blushed, then laughed and blushed again; but, without waiting to be bidden a second time, tripped up to me, gave me both her hands, and saying, "Cousin Ikey, how do you do?" with a voice that was charming in every word save one—the infernal "Ikey"—she very innocently turned her cheek up to be saluted.

I felt myself called upon to give her a lesson in politeness, and therefore put my lips to her hand, saying, Cousin P—P—Pattie—ehem, the girls will all call her petty-patty—Petty-patty Wilkins—I beg your pardon; but it is quite ungenteel and vulgar to kiss a lady; that is to say, in common cases. But— "As I spoke, I admired her beauty the more, and began to think the etiquette in such cases was absurd—But, as we are cousins, I think that alters the case entirely."

And with that I paid my respects to her cheek, and, upon my soul, was rather gratified than otherwise. Nay, and upon an instinct which I know not whether I owed to my soul or body, I made an offer to repeat the ceremony, that I might be as condescending as possible; when the little minx, to my surprise and indignation, lifted up one of the hands I had dropped, and absolutely boxed me on the ear, starting away at the same time, and saying, with a most mischievous look of retaliation,

"I reckon I know manners as well as anybody."

"Ged, and upon my soul!" said I, and marched up to the glass to restore my left whisker to its beauty, for she had knocked it out of its equilibrium, while my uncle Wilkins fell foul of her, and scolded her roundly for her bad behaviour.

"It don't signify, pa," said the amiable Pattie, bursting into tears, "I served cousin Ikey no worse than cousin Ikey served me; for when I wanted him to kiss me he wouldn't; and if he had boxed my ear it wouldn't have been half so bad; for it was very rude of him not to kiss me, and say it was vulgar, and he can't deny it."

I have mentioned before, I think, the surprising facility women seem to have of turning the tables upon a man, in any contest that may happen between the sexes; for, let a man be never so much in the right, my head for it, the woman will soon prove him to be in the wrong.

I found the truth of the maxim on the present occasion; for there was the pretty Pattie, who had just shocked my sensibilities, wounded my self-love, violated my dignity, and disordered my whisker, by a buffet on the cheek, extremely well laid on, considering the youth and sex of the bestower, now weeping and bewailing the injury I had done her, in moralizing over a kiss before taking it. It occurred to me she was an uncommon goose; but she looked so wonderfully handsome, pouting her lips with such a beautiful pettishness, that I was convinced I had treated her very badly; for which reason I stepped up to her, and begged her pardon so penitently, that she relented and forgave me, and we were soon in a good-humour with one another.

She seemed to me to be an odd creature, disposed to be whimsical and funny, and I rather feared she was, at bottom, witty. I say, I feared she was witty; and lest the reader should draw wrong inferences from the expression, I think it right to inform him, that, while recording my adventures in the body of Mr. I. D. Dawkins, I feel my old Dawkins habits revived so strongly in my feelings, that I cannot avoid giving some of the colouring of his character to the history of his body. I do not presume to say what women should be, or what they should not: in confessing a fear that my cousin Pattie was witty, I only record the horror with which I, while a dandy, in common with all others of the class, regarded any of the sex who were smarter or more sensible than myself.

My cousin Pattie was, then, odd, whimsical, and, I feared, witty; but that remained to be proved. She certainly acted in a manner highly unsophisticated, which arose from her youth (for my uncle told me she was not yet eighteen), and her country breeding. She had divers rusticities of speech, and a frankness of spirit that would at any moment burst out in weeping and wailing, or a fit of romping; all which was horridly ungenteel, and a great objection to genteel people taking notice of her.

But, on the other hand, she was a positive beauty; and although she slouched about sometimes, when forgetful, her movements were commonly graceful and lady-like.

My judgment was therefore favourable: beauty, grace, good clothes, and a grammatical way of speaking, were, as far as I knew, the only requisites for a fine woman, and I thought it was possible to make her one. The two first requisites she already possessed: good clothes were to be had of a good milliner; and as for her conversation, I flattered myself I could, in a few lessons, teach her to subdue all redundances; for in that particular she wanted nothing but pruning.

CHAPTER XIII.

A FURTHER ACCOUNT OF MISS PATTIE WILKINS.

Having made these observations in the course of a ten minutes conversation, I perceived I had no longer any reason to be ashamed of her; but, on the contrary, to congratulate myself on the relationship. Then, permitting myself to be affectionate and frank, as a near kinsman should, I gave her freely to understand, that, with a little advice and training, which I would undertake to give her in a few lessons, she would be fit to shine in the very best society: an admission that set my uncle into an ecstasy of delight and triumph, while it somewhat discomposed the fair Pattie. She gave me a hearty stare (a thing I was glad to see, for it looked lady-like), then coloured (a circumstance I did not approve so much, since blushing is girlish and ungenteel), and then burst out a laughing, and concluded by seizing upon my hand, giving it a yeomanly shake, and saying,

"Very well, cousin Ikey, you shall be my schoolmaster, and teach me all you know; and, as you say, I think you can teach me in a very few lessons."

And here she looked as meek, and quiet, and almost as sanctimonious, as any saint I ever saw of a Sunday.

"Very good," said I; "and the first lesson I will give you is, never to call me 'Ikey' again, for that's vulgar; but always 'Mr. Dawkins,' or just plain 'cousin;' or, as we are so nearly related, why, I don't care if you call me by my middle name, 'Dulmer.'"

"Wouldn't 'Dully' be better?" said she, as sweetly as could be: "it's more affectionate, and cousins ought to be affectionate."

"That's very true," said I; and, upon my soul, I thought her mouth was the handsomest I had ever seen; "it is very true, but it don't do to be too familiar; and, besides, Dully don't sound a whit better than Pattie. I wish to ged you had a better name than *that*; and yet it is the best of them all, for 'Martha' is kitchen-like, and 'Abigail' wash-womanly—"

"And Pat," said my cousin—

"*Pat!*" said I, struck with horror—

"Yes, Pat!" said she, looking as if she would cry again; "it is the most odious of nicknames, and there's my brother Sam, who calls me so all day long; and there's pa, who is not much better. But I say, cousin, I hope you'll take *them* to schooling too. I won't say any thing about pa; but I reckon there's none of us will be the worse for a little rubbing up."

"Don't say 'reckon,'" said I, "nor 'Sam' neither. Ged, you have horrid names among you, but we'll do the best we can. Pattie—Miss Pattie Wilkins; well, the name is not so very bad. As for your brother, you must always call him 'brother;' occasionally you may say 'Wilkins,' and it will sound aristocratic, as being a family name. But I say, uncle, we can't do any thing till we have you in your own house; and, if you mean to pass for a man of quality, it must be a grand one—that is, as grand as can be had without building. I say, uncle, if you please, what do you hold yourself worth?"

"Ods bobs!" said my uncle, bristling up, "what's that any man's business? Never blab a man's capital, for—"

"Oh," said Pattie, "Pa's always thinking about trade and shop-keeping; but I'll tell you, for I know all about it, for he told me six months ago, and I know. He's worth two—" and here the little beauty looked as if she designed to make me her confidant at once, and swell my very soul with the greatness of her revealment—"he's worth two hundred and ninety thousand dollars; and when he dies he is to leave me half. A'n't it grand?"

"To leave you *half!* one hundred and forty-five thousand dollars?" said I, so confounded by a sudden idea that entered my mind that I could not even conceal it. "Hang it, if that's the case, but I shall certainly marry you, and snap up that hundred and forty-five myself."

"*Would* you?" said the imp, looking so lovely, and innocent, and willing that I positively threw my arms around her neck, as if the matter were already settled.

"Ods bobs!" said my uncle, "none of your jokes here, nevvy!"

As for Pattie, she jumped out of my arms, though apparently more pleased with the rudeness than with my former want of enthusiasm, and ran laughing to a chair.

"None of your jokes here, nevvy, I say," cried Mr. Wilkins; "and don't talk to Pattie about marrying, for she has had enough of that already."

"I ha'n't, pa," said the daughter, beginning to cry again; "you're always twitting me with Danny. But I'm sure, if you're willing, I'd as lief marry my cousin Ikey—that is, cousin Dulmer—as anybody."

"Who's Danny?" said I.

My uncle looked black, but Pattie answered boldly,

"Why, my sweetheart, to be sure—Danny Baker—one of the truest sweethearts you ever saw; and oh, so handsome! But he was nothing but one of pa's clerks, and so we turned him off between us; and because I took his part, and said it was no great harm in him to like me, pa is always twitting me about him, and I can't abide it. If I am to be twitted about everybody that likes me, I should like to know where will be the end of it?"

I perceived that my little cousin had a good opinion of herself, which was proper enough; but I reprobated the good-will she extended to her admirer, telling her that all clodhoppers were to be despised, and that she must now think of being liked by none but fine gentlemen. My counsel, as I discovered afterward, was peculiarly acceptable to my uncle, and greatly increased his respect for me; and as for Pattie, she dried her eyes, and said "she had as much spirit as anybody, but Danny Baker was no fool, for all we might say of him."

In short, the interview was much more satisfactory than I had dared to anticipate; and finding my uncle and cousin were eager to have my instructions and assistance, so as to begin the world as soon and with as much eclat as possible, I summoned my wisdom, and laid down the law to them forthwith. A house was to be immediately had; and recollecting the state of Mr. Periwinkle Smith's affairs, I recommended that my uncle should make proposals for his dwelling, which was just the house required, and which I supposed Mr. Smith, or the sheriff for him, would soon bring to the hammer. Nay, in the exuberance of my affection, I offered to begin the negotiation myself, and visit Mr. Periwinkle Smith that day; whereby I might have an opportunity to return my thanks for his friendly assistance at the Schuylkill, without exciting any false hopes in the bosom of his daughter, which I feared might be the result if I went without an object.

I then discoursed on the subject of carriages and horses, furniture, tailors, and mantuamakers, and with such effect, that I perceived I should have the control of all my uncle's affairs, directing his expenses, and making all his purchases; which I saw would be highly advantageous in reinstating my credit, even if it led to no better profit.

CHAPTER XIV.

A SHORT CHAPTER, CONTAINING AN ACCOUNT OF THE AUTHOR'S COUSIN, SAMUEL WILKINS, JR.

Having debated these matters to my satisfaction and theirs, I was about taking my leave, when my cousin Sammy unexpectedly entered the apartment.

His appearance struck me dumb, and filled me with mingled terror and despair. What could I do with such a scarecrow? His appearance was death to my hopes of making the family fashionable. He was a raw youth of twenty or twenty-one, but six feet high, long-legged, lantern-jawed, and round-shouldered. He wore a white hat, like his father, but stuck upon his head with a happy contempt of order and symmetry; and his coat hung down in a straight line from his shoulders, as if cut to fit the wall of a house. He walked with a lazy, grave swagger, indicative of vast serenity of mind and self-regard, and—until I cured him of the habit—with both hands in his pockets. There was not an ounce of brain in his whole head, big as it was; though, from the gravity with which he stared and whistled one in the face (for staring and whistling were two of his greatest characteristics), it might have been supposed otherwise. I will not say the clown was ugly in visage or deformed in person; but he was a slouch from head to foot. One could see at a look that he considered himself a gentleman, that he lived in the country, and that the highest exercise of his gentility had been to stalk about from one mud-hole to another, with his hands in his pockets.

He did not seem at all daunted by my appearance, but, having surveyed me with his great staring eyes, he dragged one of his fists out of his pocket and gave me a friendly grasp, very much like the pinch of a bear. "Glad to see you; hope you're well," he said, and said no more, but remained observing me with extreme gravity during the remainder of the conference. When I got up to depart he rose also, and, though I could have well dispensed with such an escort, attended me to the door. He uttered not a word until we came within view of the bar, when the great oaf opened his lips, and said, with an extremely knowing look, "I say, Ikey, my boy, suppose we take a smaller?"

"A *smaller*!" said I, indignantly; "gentlemen in a city never drink smallers."

"Well, then," said the goose, "I don't care if we go the whole gill."

"Come," said I, commiserating his ignorance, "you must never more talk of such things. None but vulgarians drink strong liquors; slings, cocktails, and even julaps are fit only for bullies. Gentlemen never drink any thing but wine."

"Wine's small stuff," said my kinsman, with great equanimity; "but I'm for any thing that's genteel, and dad says you're the boy for showing us. But, od rabbit it, it's a hard thing to play the gentleman in a place where you a'n't up to it; but I say, now, how do you think we'll do—me and Pat?"

I could scarce avoid laughing in the booby's face, he asked his question with such simplicity and complacency. I perceived that, notwithstanding his lazy serenity and stolid gravity, he was as anxious to be made genteel as either of the others, and quite as ready to submit to my guidance. I told him I had no doubt he would do very well when I had polished him a little, which I would soon do; and I resolved to begin the task without delay. I carried him to a private apartment, ordered a carriage, and a bottle of Chateau-Margaux to amuse us while it was getting ready, and gave him to understand I would immediately take him to a tailor's; and this I did in a very short time, to the infinite delight of my friend Snip, whom I ordered to make three or four different suits for him, without troubling myself to ask his opinion about either. I then carried him in the same way to a hatter, shoemaker, and man-milliner, leaving the jeweller, watchmaker, and so on, for a future occasion.

These important matters being accomplished, greatly to my own advantage, for I took care to speak of my uncle Wilkins in a way to produce the strongest effect, I ordered the coachman to drive up to Mr. Periwinkle Smith's, whither I thought I might as well proceed while I had a coach to carry me. I gave my gawky cousin to understand my business was to buy the house for his father, at which he expressed much satisfaction (for everybody in Philadelphia knows the house is a very fine one), and a desire to help me examine it; but telling him there were many fine ladies there, who must not see him till he was properly dressed, I charged him to wait for me in the coach until I returned.

CHAPTER XV.

IN WHICH SHEPPARD LEE VISITS MR. PERIWINKLE SMITH AND HIS FAIR DAUGHTER, AND IS INTRUSTED WITH A SECRET WHICH BOTH ASTONISHES AND AFFLICTS HIM.

———

I pulled the bell with a most dignified jerk, and asked for Mr. Smith. But the servant, who grinned with approbation as at an old acquaintance, and doubtless considered that he knew more about the matter than myself, as Philadelphia servants usually do, ushered me into the presence of Mr. Smith's fair daughter.

"Ah!" said I to myself, as I cast my eye around the apartment, and saw that her levee consisted of but a single beau—a stranger whom I did not know, but who, I learned afterward, was a young millionaire from Boston—"the world begins to suspect the mortgages, and friends are falling away. Poor dear Miss Smith!"—And I felt great compassion for her.

She seemed somewhat surprised at my appearance, and I thought she looked confused. She was a marvellous fine creature, and I was quite sorry she was not rich.

I saw she had a sneaking kindness for me yet; but it was not right to encourage her. I hastened, therefore, to express my thanks for the sympathy which I had been informed she had bestowed on me, on the memorable occasion of my dip in the Schuylkill; and regretted that the indisposition consequent upon that disaster had prevented my calling earlier. I had not met the fair lady at Mrs. Pickup's or the Misses Oldstyle's, or at the other two place where I had figured during the last four evenings; and although it was highly probable she knew my indisposition had not prevented my going to these places, yet my not seeing her made the excuse perfectly genteel and fair. Yet she looked at me intently—I thought sadly and reproachfully—for a moment, and then, recovering herself, expressed her pleasure to see me so well restored, and ended, with great self-possession, by presenting me to her new admirer. After this her manner was cooler, and I thought her pique rendered her a little neglectful. It was certain she wished me to observe that she had a high opinion of the new Philander; a circumstance to which I was not so indifferent as I ought to have been. But, in truth, she was an elegant soul, and the more I looked at her the more I regretted she was not a fortune. I felt myself growing sentimental, and, to check the feeling, I resolved to proceed to business.

I had no sooner asked after the old gentleman, and expressed a desire to see him, than she gave me a look that bewildered me. It expressed surprise and inquiry, mingled with what I should have fancied contempt, could I have believed anybody could entertain such a feeling for me. She rang the bell, ordered my desire to be conveyed to her father, and in a few moments I was requested to walk up stairs to his study, where I found him in company with a gentleman of the law and a broker, whose face I knew, and surrounded with papers.

"Ah!" said I to myself, "things are now coming to a crisis; he is making an assignment."

The gentleman of the law and the broker took their departure, and Mr. Periwinkle Smith gave me a hard look. I began to suspect what he was thinking of; he was perhaps looking for me to make a declaration in relation to his fair daughter.

That he might not be troubled with such expectation long, I instantly opened my business, and gave him to understand I came to make proposals (he opened his eyes and grinned) for his house (he looked astounded), which, I had heard, he was about to dispose of.

"Indeed!" said he, and then fell to musing a while. "Pray, Mr. Dawkins," said he, "who sent you upon this wise errand?"

I did not like his tone, but I answered I came on the part of my uncle, Samuel Wilkins, of Wilkinsbury Hall—for I thought it as well to make my kinsman's name sound lordly.

"Very good," said he; "but what made you suppose I intended to sell my property?"

I liked this question still less than the other, and mumbled out something about common report, "and the general talk of my acquaintance."

"Ah!" said he, "now I understand," giving me a grin which I did not. "Let us be frank with one another. There was something said about 'mortgages,' was there not?—a heavy weight on my poor estate?"

Thinking it was useless to mince the matter, I acknowledged that such was the report.

"And it is from the influence of that report I am to understand some of the peculiarities of your—that is to say, it is to that I am to attribute your present application? Really, Mr. Dawkins, I am afraid I can't oblige you; my house I like very well, and—But I'll admit you to a little secret;" and smiling with great suavity, he laid his hand on a pile of papers. "Here," said he, "are mortgages, and other bonds, to the amount of some seventy thousand dollars; they are my property, and not mortgages on my property. The truth is (and, as you are an old friend, I don't scruple to tell you), that having a little loose cash which I did not know what to do with, I took the advice of a friend, and invested it in the form in which you now see it, and I believe it is very safe. The story of the mortgages was quite true, only it was told the wrong way."

I was petrified, and stood staring on the old gentleman with awe and amazement.

"Some people," said he, very good-naturedly, "might doubt the propriety, and even the honourableness, of a private gentleman investing money in this way; but stocks are at a high premium, and many unsafe, and money can't lie idle:—I hope you are satisfied: I am quite sorry I can't oblige your uncle. My house, as I said, I like extremely well; and I have, besides, promised it as a wedding-present to my daughter."

Oh, ye gods of Greece and Rome! a wedding-present to his daughter! I resolved to make her a proposal without delay, and I thought I might as well break matters to the old gentleman.

"Your daughter," said I, "your beloved and excellent daughter—"

"Will doubtless always be happy to welcome her old friend and admirer, Mr. Dawkins," said he; and I thought he looked beautiful—though I never thought so before. He could not have spoken more plainly, I thought, if he had said "marry her," at once. I took my leave, intending to make love to her on the spot.

"I will have the pleasure to see you to the door," said the old gentleman, and to the door he *did* see me. I do not well know how it happened; but instead of entering the parlour again, I found myself led to the front door by the courteous Mr. Smith, and bowed handsomely out, to the great satisfaction of my cousin Sammy, who regarded proceedings from the carriage window.

"Good morning," said Mr. Periwinkle Smith; "I can't sell my daughter's house, but I should be glad to have you for a neighbour; and, now I recollect it, there's Higginson the brewer's house over the way there advertised for sale, and I am told it is very well finished."

"So am *I*," said I to myself, as the door closed on my face—"finished unutterably." It occurred to me I was turned out of the house; and the suspicion was soon very perfectly confirmed. I called on the fair Miss Smith the next day, and, though I saw her by accident through the window, I was met by the cursed fib—"not at home." The same thing was told me seven days in succession, and on the eighth I saw, to my eternal wo and despair, her marriage with my Boston rival announced in the papers. He lives in Philadelphia, and can confirm my story. But this is anticipating my narrative.

"I say, Dawkins," cried my cousin Sammy (I had cured him of the vulgar 'Ikey'), "what does the old codger say?"

These words, bawled by the rustic from the carriage window, woke me from a trance into which I had fallen, the moment Mr. Periwinkle Smith shut the door in my face.

"Didn't he say there was a house over the way?"

I remembered the words,—my own house for sale! I knew it well; it was just the thing wanted,—an elegant house, provided genteel people were in it. I was on the point of running over and securing it, when I remembered Mrs. Higginson. A cold sweat bedewed my limbs. "No!" said I, "I will go to Tim Doolittle—I can face *him*."

To make matters short—for I have a long story to tell—I drove up to Higginson's brewery (it is now Doolittle and Snagg's, or was, when I heard last of it), saw my late brother-in-law, whom I thought a very plebeian body, and made such progress with him, that in three days' time (for my Margaret had gone to mourn in the country) the house changed owners, and my uncle Wilkins marched into it as master, followed by Sammy and Pattie.

CHAPTER XVI.

CONTAINING MUCH INSTRUCTIVE MATTER IN RELATION TO GOOD SOCIETY, WHEREBY THE AMBITIOUS READER CAN DETERMINE WHAT ARE HIS PROSPECTS OF ENTERING IT.

Three days after I had established my uncle in his new house, the fair Miss Smith was married.

It was a great blow to me, and I mused with melancholy on the fickleness of the sex, wondering what it was in woman's nature that enabled her so easily to change from one love to another. I considered myself very badly used; and the more I thought of the wedding-present, and the seventy thousand dollars in bonds and mortgages, the more deeply did I feel my loss. I read the announcement of her marriage in the newspaper, cursed her inconstancy and hard-heartedness, and gave myself up to grief the whole morning. She had certainly used me ill, but by dinner-time I remembered I had served her pretty much in the same way.

Besides, my cousin Pattie (I always dined with my uncle Wilkins, of course, and intended soon to live with him altogether) looked uncommonly handsome, and "Who knows," said I to myself, "whether she won't have *more* than Miss Smith, after all?" In addition to this great consolation, I had another in a few days; and the two together quite comforted me for the loss of Periwinkle's daughter. But of this in its place.

In three days' time, as I have mentioned, I had my uncle Wilkins in his new house, and was busy polishing the family. But the task was harder than I supposed. The rusticities of my uncle were inveterate; and as for Sammy, the only change I could effect in him was such as the tailor effected for me. I found him a clown, and a clown I left him. I should have given him up after the first day, had it not been that his father kept him pretty well supplied with pocket-money; which was an advantage to me, for I never could borrow any thing of my uncle. I therefore treated him civilly, and carried him about to divers places, taking good care, however, that he should not fall into the hands of my friend Tickle, or any other poor dandy.

My cousin Pattie was more docile; and I perceived that as soon as I should cure her of a mischievous habit she had of playing tricks upon everybody in the house, and myself too, upon occasions, she would be fit for any society.

As soon as my uncle had procured a carriage, (and I took care it should be a good one—I made an effort to buy my fine old thousand-dollar bays, but Mr. Doolittle would not part with them), I took her out airing and shopping, to teach her how to behave in public; and I contracted with Mrs. Pickup, who lived close by, and who it was supposed, on account of her six balls, would make a favourable sensation, to chaperon her for the season. I took care to bestow her patronage among the aunts and sisters of my tradespeople in such a way as to advance my own credit; and thinking it would be to my advantage to have such a friend near her, I recommended Nora Magee to her for a maid, although Nora was not quite so genteel as I should have wished.

In short, I did every thing that was proper to prepare her way for the approaching season; and as soon as I thought her fit to receive company, went round among all the leading fashionables, and requested them to visit her.

It was here that the invaluable nature of my services on behalf of my country kinsfolk was shown, as I took care to make them understand; for without me to help them, or some other equally genteel person, my uncle and cousins might as well have tried to get into Congress as into good society. My request was not granted until I had answered ten thousand different questions, and removed as many scruples, on the part of the monarchs of the mode. There were a thousand reasons why my uncle's family should be denied admission into that elegant society they were so ambitious to enter; and nothing but the force of my recommendations ensured them success.

My labours on this occasion made me familiar with the principles upon which republican aristocratic society is founded; and as these principles are not universally understood, even in America, I think I can do nothing better than explain them, for the benefit of all my young and aspiring readers.

The pretensions of any individual to enter the best society of the republic depend upon his respectability; and the measure of this is determined by the character of his profession, if he have one—if not, by that of his father. I never knew even the most exclusive and fastidious of examiners to carry his scrutiny so far back as a grandfather; for, indeed, all our grandfathers in America were pretty much alike, and the sooner we forget them the better.

The first profession in point of dignity is that of a gentleman, who has nothing to do but to spend his revenue, if he has one. There are some gentlemen well received in good society who live upon their wits; but they are born in it. Poor gentlemen, not already in society, had better not try to get into it; for rich men who have romantic daughters are afraid of them. A gentleman, then, always stands a fair chance of being admitted; and if his father was of a respectable profession, he is received with open arms. The preference accorded to this class is just, since founded upon nature. All occupations are more or less disgraceful; a strong proof of which is found in the fact that all primitive nations, such as the Hottentots, and North American Indians, look upon them with contempt, considering idleness and war as the only business for gentlemen. Providence, indeed, ordained that men should live by the sweat of their brows; but it is horrid ungenteel to do so.

The next profession in point of dignity is law; and lawyers, as I may say, form the true effective nobility of America; for though the mere gentlemen deem themselves higher and purer, they are pretty generally considered by others as only the lady-dowagers of society. But the lady-dowagers sometimes consider the gentility of lawyers doubtful.

The third profession is that of arms, which owes its consideration mainly to the women; who, although the ministers of love and mercy to man, are wondrous fond of those who deal in blood and gunpowder. These are the only respectable professions in America.

Divinity, physic, merchandise, agriculture, and politics, are the only others from which a man is occasionally allowed to enter good society. But they are considered low, and it is only peculiar circumstances which can give any of their followers a claim to rise.

I have said that the claim of the gentlemen to consider themselves the highest class is founded in nature. They form the nucleus of society, and around them, as they are admitted, the members of the other professions establish the grand order of fashion. According to their creed, law is a respectable profession, because it keeps down the mob, or people, by keeping them constantly by the ears, and because it makes money; and arms they hold to be reputable, because it does the same thing, and paves the way to the presidency. Divinity and physic they consider to be naturally low occupations, since their provinces are only to take care of dirty souls and bodies. Merchandise is denounced, since it consists of both buying and selling, whereas, buying is the only part of traffic that is fit for a gentleman. Agriculture is contemned, because there are so many clodhoppers engaged in it; and politics, because it demands consociation with the mob.

In these five professions, however, certain fortunate circumstances may give a claim to notice. Parsons (who are often doctors of divinity and always reverends) and physicians are titled gentry, and this counts in their favour; and the same thing may be said of politicians, when they rise to be secretaries of departments or foreign ministers, or become renowned as orators: great distinction will secure them favour, for they are then people that people look at. Merchants are allowed to be respectable as soon as they are worth a million, provided they have two or three daughters and no sons, and are willing to be splendid in their entertainments. An agriculturist of our own latitudes can never expect to be made respectable; but a planter of cotton or tobacco, who owns a hundred negroes, and puts the name of his farm or the county he lives in after his own, has as good a chance as any.

All other classes are vulgar and mechanical, and therefore ineligible. Men of science and genius are excluded on account of their manners, which are outlandish, and their arrogant display of superiority, which is disagreeable; and as for the actors, dancers, and singers that are sometimes met with, the two first are admitted, because they are foreign and famous, and the last, because they bring good music for nothing.

From this exposition of the code of society, it will be seen that my uncle Wilkins could boast but slender claims to an introduction. His occupation had been vulgar, and he had not made money enough to ennoble him. I trebled his two hundred and ninety thousand, as is usual, but I could not deny that his son was named Sammy, and his daughter Pattie.

But what spoke highly in his favour was, that whatever had been his profession, he had now abandoned it, with the praiseworthy intention of living a gentleman during the remainder of his life; and what was also advantageous, he had pursued it at such a distance from the haunts of fashion that his new friends might, with the greatest propriety, affect an entire ignorance of it.

His having a daughter, too, and but one son to divide with her his eight hundred and seventy thousand—that is to say, his two hundred and ninety—was also a strong recommendation to those mammas who had sons to provide for; and his determination to indulge the fair Pattie in as many balls and parties as she desired, was another circumstance to propitiate favour.

But, to crown all, *I* countenanced him; and that settled the matter. In a few days' time there was such a rattle and trampling at the brewer's door as had never been known before. The whole square was in commotion, being choked up with carriages; and such was the throng of genteel people rushing into the house, that an unsophisticated dealer in second-hand furniture, supposing there was an auction to be held, stalked into the parlour, and electrified everybody by wondering, in the way of a question not addressed to any particular person, "when the sale was to begin?"

In short, the thing was settled; my uncle was dubbed a gentleman, and every occurrence went to show that in the approaching season his rank would be confirmed, and his daughter recognised as a belle by everybody in town.

But before that time a change came o'er the spirit of my fate, and—But I shall confess the whole affair to the reader.

CHAPTER XVII.

IN WHICH SHEPPARD LEE RELATES THE PASSION HE CONCEIVED FOR HIS FAIR COUSIN, AND HIS ENGAGEMENT TO ELOPE WITH HER.

My uncle Wilkins, it seems, was not merely ambitious to get into good society; he was ambitious to have his daughter married, and, as he said, into the best family in the land: an object not very difficult to compass, considering the fortune he intended to leave her. But my uncle was resolved her husband should be rich as well as distinguished; and I discovered the old curmudgeon had an extreme horror of poverty. Perhaps one of the strongest reasons for his leaving the country was a fear he had lest his adorable daughter should be snapped up by that aforesaid Danny Baker, whom my cousin had pronounced "one of the truest and handsomest sweethearts I ever saw;" although I never saw him at all, nor, indeed, any other extremely true and handsome sweetheart of the male gender in all my life; for those that are true are ugly, and those that are handsome are as uncertain as politics. I say this was my uncle's fear, and, indeed, he confessed to me his belief that Pattie had really a sneaking kindness for the young rustic; for which reason he was anxious to have her married as soon as possible.

I may here observe, that if a bachelor is to judge of the excellence of love by the character of its vocabulary, he will discover no stirring reason to lament his insensibility. All the expressions on the subject go to show that there is something mean and contemptible in the tender passion, which men otherwise profess to be the most heavenly of the passions—as if, indeed, heaven had any thing to do with any of them. The moment a man begins to think a woman uncommonly charming, he is said to cast a "sheep's eye" on her; when he feels a friendship for her, it becomes "a sneaking kindness;" and the moment his heart is in a hubbub, he is "deep in the mire." From these terms, and others that might be mentioned, it results as I have said, namely—that men and women who have experienced the tender passion, are, notwithstanding their pretences to the contrary, really ashamed of it; that a lover is a sheep and a sneaking fellow, ordained to grovel in the mud at the feet of his mistress; and, finally, that a bachelor has no good reason to execrate his stars for keeping him single.

But I had other notions when I was in Mr. I. D. Dawkins's body.

I was entirely of my uncle's way of thinking, and proposed to take her myself; to which my uncle replied, in some perturbation, "None of your jokes there, Ikey, my boy;" and gave me plainly to understand that was a thing he would never think of. Nay, the proposition seemed to him so unpalatable, that I was compelled to pretend I had made it entirely in jest; though I demanded, supposing I had been serious, what objection he could have to me. "Oh, none in the world," said he, "except your being so near of blood; for a cousin-german is almost the same as a brother."

I understood the old hunks better than he thought; he had, somehow or other, found out that I had spent my fortune, and was therefore, in that particular, no better off than Mr. Danny Baker. I saw, too, clearly enough, that he only valued me as a sort of stepping-stone into society; and that, having once had all the advantage of me he could, he would be ready to forget all my benefits. The curmudgeon! he had found out I had been borrowing money of his son Sammy, and he was already longing for the time to come when he might safely discard me.

I resolved to marry Pattie in spite of him; and began to cast about for some device by which to secure her share of his two hundred and ninety thousand, which it was more than probable he would withhold, in the event of her marrying against his will. This device I soon hit upon.

I told him there was, among all my acquaintance, not above one man whom I could recommend as a husband for Pattie; for though there were dozens of genteel young fellows, fortunes were by no means so plentiful. My friend Tickle, I assured him, was just the man,—a little gay, to be sure; indeed, quite dissipated; and, what was worse, an enemy to matrimony; which was the more extraordinary, as by marrying he might come at once into possession of a splendid fortune. And thereupon I told him that Jack's father, who was a saint in his way, and a bigot, to reclaim him, had, by will (for I assured him the poor man was dead), bequeathed his superb estate to him only upon condition that he married before the expiration of five years; failing in which, the whole property, now in the hands of trustees, would revert to other persons, with the exception of a shabby annuity of a thousand a year. The five years, I told my uncle Wilkins, were now nearly expired, and Jack, being in some alarm, was already expressing an inclination to seek a spouse; but she must be a rich one, otherwise he would never think of her.

This story, which I fabricated for the purpose, produced a strong effect upon my uncle Wilkins; and I concluded it by recommending he should without delay settle half his fortune upon Pattie, by legal grant of *dedi et concessi*, as the lawyers call it, and register the same; in which event, I would do all I could to bring the marriage about, not doubting that we should succeed, since Pattie was, as I averred, just the sort of girl that Tickle liked.

My uncle was rather dumbfounded at the last proposal, and swore he would do no such thing. "He was not going," he said, "to bribe anybody to take his girl off his hands, not he; she should have her share when he was dead, and if she married to his liking, why she should have something before. I might bring my friend Tickle to see her if I would, and he would see what he thought of him."

My uncle put a bold face upon the matter, but I perceived he was eager to make the acquaintance of my friend Tickle, and would be soon brought to reason. And, indeed, after having seen the intended son-in-law, and listened some half a dozen times over to my arguments, he opened his heart so far as to settle the sum of forty thousand dollars upon Pattie, which—or rather the yearly interest of that sum, for the crafty old sly-boots took care to constitute himself trustee for the girl, and retain the principal in his own hands—he conditioned to pay her after her marriage.

I was provoked at his stinginess; but as no better terms could be had, I thought I might as well bring the matter to a conclusion, trusting that something better would turn up after my marriage.

I say *my* marriage, for I had no thoughts of bestowing forty thousand dollars, or the interest thereof, upon my friend Tickle. I made him my confidant in the matter, and easily prevailed upon him to assist me in deceiving my uncle Wilkins, by appearing to Pattie in the light of a wooer. As for Pattie herself, who, I was persuaded, had fallen in love with me at first sight, I made her a declaration, which diverted and delighted her beyond expression; and revealing to her also my project to secure her an independence, she agreed to do her part in the play, pretend a great fancy for Mr. Tickle, and run away with me, the moment her father should make her the grant in question.

The grant *was* made, as I mentioned before; but by that time I was in a dilemma, having made an engagement to elope with another lady, who was in some respects highly attractive, and had fallen devouringly in love with me. Indeed, I may say, she made me the first offer, though it was not leap-year; but her situation excused her, especially as it was I she made love to. She was, the reader will be surprised to learn, the daughter of old Skinner, or Goldfist, the usurer; and she was rather handsome than otherwise. The engagement was brought about as will be shown in the next chapter.

CHAPTER XVIII.

IN WHICH SHEPPARD LEE RECOUNTS AN ENGAGEMENT OF A SIMILAR NATURE WHICH HE FORMED WITH THE FAIR ALICIA.

My creditors, looking with great certainty for their money, now that my long-talked-of uncle had got to town, having waited a couple of weeks for payment in vain, began to besiege me in a highly importunate way; and as no assistance was to be had of my uncle, and Sammy's purse was not so well filled as I could have wished, I was reduced to great straits.

Conversing on this subject with my friend Tickle, he advised me to visit old Goldfist, as I (that is, my prototype, the true Dawkins) had often done before, and see what could be had out of him on the strength of my projected nuptials.

The advice being as good as could be had (for Tickle's pockets were as empty as my own), I proceeded to the old fellow's house after nightfall—for I did not care to be observed.

Having knocked at the door, it was opened by no less a person than Skinner's fair daughter herself, as I soon discovered; and, in fact, I had some faint recollection of having seen her before. There was a lamp on the pavement before the door, by which I could see her very plainly. She blushed, and smiled, and looked confused, and when I asked for her father, made me some answer which I did not understand; but, as she invited me to enter, I followed her into the house, expecting to be led to the money-lender. She conducted me, however, to a parlour, not over and above well furnished, for Skinner was a notorious skinflint, when, having vouchsafed to converse with her a while, I again asked after her father.

She told me he was not at home; but seeing me rise to depart, she stammered out an assurance that he would soon return; which caused me to resume my seat, evidently to her great pleasure.

Seeing this, I condescended to make myself agreeable, and with such effect, that the simple-hearted foolish creature began to tell me how often she had seen me at her father's house a year or two before, when she was a little school-girl, as she said, and how glad she was to see me back again; as if, a year or two before, we had been intimate acquaintances; when, on the contrary, as my associations assured me, I (or my original) had never taken the slightest notice of her—as, in truth, why should I, her father being so much beneath me?

I believe I rather gave her a stare; but she looked so admiringly at me, I could do no less than continue to be agreeable; and, to tell the truth, I was afterward amazed at my condescension.

By-and-by there dropped in one of her brothers, a very fine looking young man for one of his rank in life, but of a dissipated, under-the-table look, and, I thought, somewhat *julapized*—which is a word that, among certain classes, signifies that one is not sober. However, he behaved with great decorum, and instead of taking a seat, as I expected, to make my acquaintance, he gave me a nod and a laugh, as much as to say, "I know what you're after, my boy," and went stumbling into the back part of the house.

In a few moments after there came another equally good looking, but not so obliging; for he helped himself to a seat without any ceremony, and, with just as little, proceeded to inform "me he supposed I was after dad; but dad was fast on an arbitration, and would not be home for at least three hours."

Poor Alicia, for that was her name (and in this particular she was better provided than my cousin Pattie), gave her brother an angry look; for at this announcement I got up and took my leave. She followed me, however, to the door, and told me if I would come at about eight o'clock on the following evening, I would find her papa at home; and she added, softly, that she would be glad to see me.—*She* glad to see me! poor soul!

I went, though, according to appointment; and, poor soul, she *was* glad to see me, as was plain enough, but "sorry that papa had not yet got through with that arbitration; and so I could not see him, unless I would be so good as to wait until he came home; and, if I would, it would be charity, for there was nobody in the house with her except old Barbara, the housekeeper, who was but poor company,—and, indeed, she had but poor company always, living a very lonesome life of it," &c. &c.; and she concluded by promising, if I would sit down, to play me a tune upon the piano!

She played me a tune accordingly, and horrid work she made of it; but, as she did her best, I praised her, and that pleased her. She then, to show me that she was accomplished, introduced me to divers bits of paper with colours on them, which she told me were drawings, and, as I knew but little of such things, I took her word for it; after which she exhibited some two or three dozen handsome-looking volumes in French and Italian, of which languages I knew no more than dandies in general; and for that reason I told her such things were now considered bores, and left to children and schoolmasters.

I perceived we were to have a tête-à-tête of it, and I began to suspect the lassie knew so when she invited me. When this idea entered my mind, I felt a little indignant; yet it was diverting to think of her simplicity. I thought I would amuse myself with her a little while, and unbend from the austerity of dignity, which seemed to gratify her most.

In this humour I permitted myself to be merry and easy; and having romped with her one way and another, much to her delight, I at last seized upon her, and gave her a buss; whereupon she acted pretty much as my cousin Pattie had done before her,—that is, she laughed, and blushed, and cried "Oh la!" but looking all the time any thing but incensed.

In short, my condescension affected her to that degree, that she began to treat me as her most undoubted friend; and, in the height of her confidence, informed me that she was just eighteen years old, minus two months (the very age of my cousin Pattie); that she was her father's favourite (as far as any one could be the favourite of such a curmudgeon); and that besides her fine expectations from him, she enjoyed in her own right a fortune of twenty thousand dollars—a bequest from some old aunt or other—which she would come into possession of as soon as the aforesaid two months and a few odd days had expired.

This was news that affected me very strongly; and had her father been a gentleman, all things considered, I believe I should have made her a declaration on the spot.

As it was, I felt my soul growing tender towards her; for though twenty thousand dollars was but a small sum, it was, if I could take her word for it, certain; which was not yet the case with any of my cousin Pattie's expectations. However, before I could digest the information, we were surprised by the turning of a dead-latch key in the front door, and Alicia cried, with a tone of disappointment, "Oh la! it is papa!"—And so it was.

The old gentleman looked upon the open piano, and the books and drawings upon the table, with surprise, and then upon me with uneasiness.

"Mr. Dawkins has been waiting, papa," said Alicia.

"Humph!" said old Goldfist, and pointed her to the door. She stole me a look, and, as she passed out, raised her hand archly to her lips. She was rather free, I confess; but she had lived a secluded life, and knew no better.

The old fellow gave me a sharp look, coughed phthisically twice or thrice, and then, with but little superfluous ceremony, asked me what I wanted.

"Money," said I.

"Oh, ay, always money. Who is to pay it? What's your security?"

"My uncle Wilkins," said I.

"Very good name, don't doubt," growled the bear; "the banks will take it. Don't do any business of that sort."

"Ged, faith, no," said I; "I don't come for money at six per cent., but on the old terms of usury. You know my uncle Wilkins, eh? Only two children—a fortune of eight hundred and seventy thousand dollars."

"Bah!" said the bull, "that will do for the girls and boys. Know all about him; one hundred and twenty, and half of it in railroads—good for nothing."

"Two hundred and ninety, *bona fide*," said I, "and half of it in bank-stock."

"Know all about it," said Mr. Skinner; "but what's that to you? Has a son of his own."

"And a daughter," said I, giving him a nod, which brought a Christian look into his face, and, doubtless, a Christian feeling into his hearts. I took advantage of it to inform him that she and I were about to elope, and wanted a thousand dollars to bear our expenses; assuring him also that her father was on the eve of making her a grant of fifty thousand dollars, as soon as which was done, we should be off at a moment's warning. To be brief, I told the old fellow all that was necessary for my purpose, and made so good a story of it, that I have no doubt I should have got something out of him, had not my evil genius suddenly prompted me to refer to his own daughter Alicia, and ask him what he intended to give her, over and above her own twenty thousand?

He looked as black as midnight, and asked "who told me she had such a sum?"

I saw I had alarmed him, and said I had it of a friend of mine, a very fine fellow, who thought of taking her off his hands, provided he would add twenty more to it.

"Want no fine fellows, and no friends of yours," said he, gruffly; "won't give her a cent, and has nothing of her own; all a fool's story—told you so herself—a jade's trick; never told a truth in her life."

The old miser's soul was up in arms; the prospect of being called upon in two months' space to render up the girl's portion to a son-in-law, was so much Scotch snuff thrown into his eyes; if it did not blind, it at least distracted him: and the reward I had for conjuring up the vision was my own dismissal, notwithstanding all my arguments to the contrary, with my pockets as empty as when I entered, a rude assurance that he had closed accounts with me, and a highly impertinent request that I would avoid troubling him for the future.

So I got no money of him, but his daughter fell in love with me; and the next day she sent me by the post a very tender and romantic billetdoux, in which she lamented her father's harshness and barbarity, hoped I would not think ill of her for venturing upon an apology, and concluded by informing me, with agreeable simplicity, that her father was never at home between eight and nine o'clock in the evening, when the weather was clear. From all which I understood, that she was as ready to run away with me as my cousin Pattie.

Having pondered over the matter for a while, it appeared to me proper to encourage her enthusiasm; so that, in the event of my uncle Wilkins refusing to make Pattie independent, I might be certain of a wife who could bring me something. I had many objections, indeed, to the lady's family and relations; but the latter I could easily cut in case of necessity, and the other I considered scarce worth thinking of. Her twenty thousand dollars was a strong recommendation; and there was no telling what her father might leave her, if reconciled after her marriage. I liked my cousin Pattie best; but, upon the whole, I considered it advisable to have a second string to my bow.

With this impression on my mind, I took occasion to drop in upon her the first clear evening, repeating the visit now and then, as suited my convenience, and promised to run away with her upon the first fitting occasion. And this promise I resolved to keep, provided my affairs with my cousin Pattie should render it advisable.

CHAPTER XIX.

THE INGENIOUS DEVICES WITH WHICH SHEPPARD LEE PREPARED THE WAY FOR THE ELOPEMENT.

I had scarce brought my friend Tickle upon the stage, and introduced him into my uncle's family, before my mind began to misgive me. I suspected that, instead of being content to play the stalking-horse for my sole advantage, he would take the opportunity to advance his own interest, and gain, if he could, my cousin Pattie for himself.

To remove all temptation, and bind him more closely to be faithful, I told him of my adventure with Alicia (taking care, however, to conceal her name, for I did not wish to forego my advantages in that quarter until convinced I could do so without loss), described her claim to the sixty thousand dollars (for, of course, I trebled her inheritance), and concluded by engaging to make her over to him the moment I was myself secure of Pattie, which would be the moment Pattie was secure of an independence.

Upon this promise Tickle made me a thousand protestations of friendship and disinterestedness, and I felt my mind more easy.

He acted his part, assisted by Pattie, who at my suggestion feigned suddenly to be violently in love with him, and besieged her father to the same end as myself: the old gentleman at last complied, and actually executed the deed of gift which I mentioned before; by which he secured to her the revenue accruing upon a sum of forty thousand dollars, the principal, which he retained in his own hands in trust, to revert to her at his death; and to this deed I was myself made a witness.

With these terms, as it seemed there were no better to be had, I allowed myself to be satisfied; and trusting to a final reconciliation with my uncle Wilkins to augment the dowry, I ran to my cousin Pattie and informed her of her good fortune.

She was filled with rapture, and began fairly to dance with joy; she told me I was the best and sweetest of cousins, and vowed she would love me to her dying day. Her joyous spirits fired my own, and I answered in terms equally ecstatic. In short, we agreed to elope that very night, and arranged our plan accordingly. It was agreed I should have a carriage in waiting at the corner of the street during the evening, and that Pattie, who was to feign herself unwell, as an excuse for not going to Mrs. Pickup's first ball, which was to take place that evening, should find some means to get her father out of the way; immediately after which I, having disposed of the redoubtable Sammy, by depositing him in the aforesaid Mrs. Pickup's drawing-room, was to make my appearance, and bear her in triumph to a reverend divine, previously secured for the ceremony.

Having settled all these things, and sealed our engagement with a kiss, my adorable cousin admitted me to a secret which nearly froze my blood with horror.

She informed me that my friend Tickle, disregarding all his vows of fidelity, had been busy ever since I brought him into the house besieging her on his own account; that he had taken every occasion to undermine me in her affections, by disparaging my good qualities both of soul and mind, and especially by assuring her I was a "great ass and fortune-hunter" (those were his very words); and, finally, that he had so used the power his knowledge of our secret had given him, by occasional threats of betraying it to her father, that she had been compelled to accept his addresses, and make him the same promise she had just made me—that is, to elope with him. The perfidious fellow had by some means got wind of the deed of gift; and while I was engaged in signing it, he had paid my cousin a visit with the same object as myself, and she had promised to decamp with him. Nay, at this moment the villain was engaged in securing his carriage and his parson, with the prospect of chousing me out of my wife and fortune!

My horror was, however, soon dissipated. My cousin Pattie had made the engagement only in self-defence, and she looked upon the whole affair as the best joke in the world. "How we will cheat him," said she; "the base fellow!" and she danced about, smiling, and laughing, and crying together, so that it was a delight to see her. "Yes," said she, with uncommon vivacity, "we will cheat him, for I'm sure he deserves no better; for I'm sure he's just as much of a goose and fortune-hunter as he said *you* were; and I'm sure I despise a goose and fortune-hunter above all things; and I'm sure I know how to treat a goose and fortune-hunter as well as anybody. How we'll laugh at him to-morrow! How he'll stare when he finds I'm gone! how papa will stare too! How Sammy will stare, and how he'll whistle! Oh dear! I *do* love to cheat people of all things; I do, cousin Ikey; and, ods fishes, I'm almost half minded to cheat you too!"

And with that she flung her arms round my neck, gave me a kiss, and ran laughing away to prepare for the hour of elopement.

There was an extraordinary coincidence between the situation of my cousin Pattie and myself. She had agreed to run away with two different people at the same moment; and so had I. The day before my uncle proved unusually crusty and self-willed, and I began to think I should never effect my point with him; and, what was equally dispiriting, I fell among duns, who persecuted me with astonishing rancour; my uncle's appearance, as it seemed, serving rather to sharpen than to allay their appetites for payment. Being thus goaded on by doubt and dunning, I resolved to make sure of Goldfist's daughter; which I did by visiting her as soon as night came, and proposing an elopement on the following evening; and this it was the more easy to put into execution, since her father, as she told me, was fast in bed with a sciatica, or some such vulgar disorder.

No one could be more willing and delighted than the fair Alicia; and it appeared that, in anticipation of the happy event, she had already made all her preparations, having, as she assured me, arranged with a friend of hers, at whose house she designed the ceremony to be performed, ordered secretly a whole trunk full of bride's clothes, and notified an old schoolmate whom she had engaged to wait upon her.

I thought, upon my soul, she was taking matters pretty easily, and acting somewhat independently; but she was ignorant of the world, as I said before, and knew no better. I was still more disgusted with the thought of being shown off among her friends, and told her a bridemaid was wholly superfluous; but she had made her mind up as to what was right on such an occasion, and I judged it proper to submit. It was agreed I should meet her at her friend's house, at nine o'clock in the evening; and "she hoped," very modestly, I thought, "that I would bring some nice pretty fellow to wait on me, that would make a good match with her dear Julia, who was the nicest dear soul in the world."

This "nice dear soul," as I afterward discovered, and as I think proper to inform the reader now, that he may understand into what a slough of democracy I was rushing, was no less a personage than a cousin-german of Mr. Snip, my tailor; and her appointment to the honour of waiting upon the bride of the distinguished I. D. Dawkins was productive of a casualty expected neither by herself nor by my adored Alicia.

I laughed in my sleeve at that hint of my Alicia; and yet I did, after all, provide myself with an attendant, and one who was perhaps better suited than any other person I could have lighted on, as an offset and pendent to the "fair Julia." This was my cousin, Sammy Wilkins; and the reason of my appointing him was this. He was, although the stupidest creature on earth, of a meddling and prying nature, and had an extraordinary fancy to go sneaking after me whithersoever I went—from admiration and affection, perhaps; but of that I was not certain; and, at all events, he was a great burden to me. He discovered my repeated visits to Skinner's house, and was seized with a stupid curiosity to know the reason; and, what was still worse, he made so many observations on my attentions to, and secret conferences with, his sister Pattie, that it was clear he suspected there was something in the wind there too. Being kept in eternal torment lest he should discover more than I liked, or, by his indiscreet tattling, awake the suspicions of others, I saw no better means of averting the mischief, and turning his eyes from his sister, than by taking him aside, and telling him, with many injunctions to secrecy, that I was courting old Skinner's rich daughter, and wished to have him wait upon me at the wedding.

Such confidence, coupled with the intention to do him so much honour, entirely overcame his rustic imaginations. He swore he approved of marrying rich wives, and was looking out for one himself, and hoped I would put him on the track of one; which I promised, and the clownish juvenile was content. He looked forward to the great event with a measure of glee I had never seen him roused to before, and he ordered a new coat of Snip, that he might do honour to his service.

It is quite true, I never really intended he should trouble himself in the matter; but when the fated evening came, when the loving Alicia, arrayed in satin and white roses, was awaiting her lover, who was preparing to run away with her rival, I thought it better to despatch him to my charmer than to leave him at Mrs. Pickup's, whence he might stray at a moment's warning, and, indeed, with no warning at all. It was quite necessary to have him out of the way; for which reason I sent him to the house where Alicia was in waiting, with a special message to the lady, to make his introduction the more easy, and a thousand instructions in relation to nothing.

It was fortunate that my cousin Sammy, though as great a rustic as ever lived, was, as little troubled with bashfulness as wisdom. Hence I found no difficulty in despatching him to my inamorata, whom he had never laid eyes on, and to her friends, with regard to whom I was in the same predicament. I promised to follow him in a short time, and thus, to my great joy, succeeded in getting him out of the way.

CHAPTER XX.

THE GUESTS THAT SHEPPARD LEE INVITED TO HIS WEDDING.

The appointed hour drew nigh, and all things had gone on swimmingly with one single exception. The persecution I had endured from Messrs. Sniggles, Snip, & Co. the day before, I was fated once more to endure; for, going home to my lodgings about dusk to put on my best shirt, I found my chief creditors assembled in solemn divan, or rather in warlike ambush; and such a troop of bears and wolves as they were was perhaps never seen by an unfortunate gentleman before. What had brought them together, especially at such an unlucky moment, it was impossible to divine; but it seems they had had in consideration the state of my affairs and prospects, and had just come to the conclusion, as I entered, that they were none the better off for the coming of my uncle Wilkins, who (for it appeared the villain Sniggles had been sounding him on the subject) had disavowed all responsibility for my debts, and all disposition to discharge them, in terms not to be mistaken. It had just been resolved, *nem. con.*, as the saying is, that I had cheated them, that I was cheating them, and that I would cheat them as long as I could, and that terms, therefore, should be kept with me no longer.

To this moment my flesh creeps when I think of the yell the villains set up when I stumbled among them, and the audacity with which they heaped on my devoted head their upbraidings, menaces, and maledictions. They used highly uncivil language, and some laid their defiling fingers upon my collar, while all, as with one voice, cried out to carry me before an alderman, and make a public spectacle of me at once.

I say my flesh yet creeps while I think of their ferocious conduct, and I shall remember it to my death-bed; for of all the various woes and grievances to which flesh is heir, and which I have had uncommon opportunities to test, there are none more truly awful in my recollections than a high case of dunning.

It was several moments before I could utter a word in defence; and when I did, having nothing better to say, I assured the rascals I was just on the eve of running away with my uncle's daughter, and of course would be soon able to answer all their scurvy demands. I told them the time was fixed, the carriage and parson prepared, and my fair Pattie in waiting; but, as I had told them many thousand things before which were not always exactly true,

I found my present assurances received with so little credit, that I was obliged to give them ocular proof of my honesty and fair-dealing. I invited them to follow me to my uncle's door, and there station themselves until they beheld me come forth conducting my bride to the carriage; after which they might, if they would, follow me in like manner to the parson: and I engaged, in the confidence of my heart, if I failed to bring out a wife according to promise, to follow them, without any further demur, to the alderman, or to old Nick himself, which was pretty much the same thing.

This proposal, being highly reasonable, was accepted; and I had the honour of such an escort to my uncle's doors as was never before enjoyed by a bridegroom. The only one who did not accompany me to my uncle's door was Mr. Snip the tailor; who, passing a house where lived, as he said, a young lady of his acquaintance, stepped in to show one of his customer's new coats that he had on, promising to follow after us in a moment. As my stars, or the father of sin, would have it, this young lady was that identical "dear Julia," his cousin-german, of whom I spoke before, and whom he found rustling in satin, just prepared, as she informed him, to join her dear Alicia Skinner, who was to be married to the handsome Mr. Dawkins, at the house of their friend Mrs. Some-one-or-other.

The tailor was thunderstruck, as tailors doubtless often are; assured the dear Julia she was mistaken, and acquainted her with the true state of the case; the result of which was, as may be understood, when she had carried her news to the expectant Alicia, a certain scene of a highly interesting nature. As for Mr. Snip himself, he rushed out of the house to bring me to an explanation; but when he reached the party I had already taken refuge in my uncle's house.

CHAPTER XXI.

CONTAINING A SCIALOGUE, OR CURIOUS CONVERSATION WITH NOTHING; WITH A DISCOVERY EXTREMELY ASTONISHING TO SEVERAL PERSONS.

I found my cousin Pattie also in her satins, and Nora Magee, whom she had resolved to take with her, decked out with extraordinary splendour; and, what I thought was diverting enough, the creature had a long bridal veil like her mistress, and as huge a cloak to conceal her person from observation. They were prepared to start, with each her bundle at hand; and they hailed my appearance with delight.

But there was a difficulty before us; my uncle Wilkins was yet in the house, and so was Sammy. As for the latter, I soon got rid of him by sending him to Alicia, as I mentioned before; but my uncle we could not remove. My cousin's affectation of sickness (to confirm which, and conceal her nuptial preparations, she kept aloof in her chamber, or pretended to do so) concerned him, and he refused to leave the house; but, being left to himself, we knew he would soon drop asleep, that being one of his rustical propensities.

By-and-by, while we were discoursing upon our difficulties, we heard a carriage drive by; and just as it passed the door, the coachman gave three loud cracks with his whip. It was a sign I had agreed upon with the fellow, and I knew all was now in readiness. I proposed that we should instantly steal down stairs, and—

At that moment I heard the front door softly open and shut.

"Who's that?" said I.

"Ah! I'm sure I don't know," said my cousin Pattie, turning so pale I thought she was going to fall down in a faint; "perhaps it is Mr. Tickle. Yes!" she cried, recovering her spirits, and almost jumping for joy,—"now we'll sort him! I'll show him how I serve fortune-hunters, I reckon! I'll lock him up in a closet, I will; and there he shall kick his heels till morning, and I don't care if the rats eat him, I don't.—Oh, goody gracious! he's coming up stairs!" she cried: "was there ever anybody so impudent? But I'll fix him. Here, cousin Ikey, do you run in here,"—pointing to her chamber,—"and don't let him see you."

"No," said I, thinking it proper to appear courageous, "I will face the faithless rascal, and punish his impertinence on the spot." I had no idea of doing any such thing, which, of course, must have alarmed my uncle, and I intended to yield to Pattie's fears and importunity, swallow my wrath for the present, and conceal myself, as she recommended. But my display of resistance awoke the indignation of Nora Magee, who cried, "Och, the divil take him thin; does he mane to rob us of our husbands?" and seizing me by the shoulders, she thrust me towards the chamber.

"Run in, cousin Ikey," said my cousin, driving the Irish barbarian away, but seizing me herself, and urging me into the chamber, while she seemed dying with suppressed mirth. "You'll see how Nora will sort him,—you'll hear it. You mustn't speak a word; and, ods fishes, you must remember to behave yourself,"—here she seemed more diverted than ever,—"ods fishes, you must behave yourself in a lady's chamber."

At that moment Nora blew out the light, so that we were left in darkness, and my cousin locked the door, thus, as I supposed, dividing us from the enemy. "I say, Pattie, my soul," said I, whispering in her ear, "what is Nora going to do with him?" But she answered me not a word, and I took that as a hint to hold my own peace. The next instant I heard a rustling in the next room, and the voice of Jack Tickle saying softly, and almost in my own words,

"I say, Pattie, my soul, what did you blow out the light for? Where are you?—Oh! you divine creature!" and I heard the smack of a kiss, that quite astonished me.

"Pattie," said I, "what the deuse is the meaning of that?"

But Pattie was as dumb as before. The rustling was transferred from the antechamber (I had taught my cousin to call it her boudoir) into the passage, and I could tell, by the creaking of a step, that my friend Tickle was going down stairs.

"Pattie," said I, "what's in the wind now?"

But still Pattie refused to answer me.

While I was wondering at her silence, now that there was no fear of being overheard, I again distinguished the sound of the house door softly opened and shut.

"I say, Pattie," said I, "what the devil is all that? and pray why don't you speak?"

It occurred to me that her silence was all owing to a fit of bashfulness, caused by her having me locked up in the chamber with her.

"Pattie," said I, reaching out my hands, "but without being able to reach her, you shouldn't be bashful nor nothing, considering we're to be married in less than half an hour. I say, Pattie, what are we to do now? where are you?"

While I spoke I heard a carriage again rattle by the door, and, to my astonishment, the coachman saluted the house with three such cracks of his whip as my own had given a few minutes before.

"Pattie," said I, while a cold sweat broke over my limbs, "*where* are you, and why don't you speak?"

I felt about the door for her, but felt in vain; I listened for the sound of her breath, hoping she might have hidden herself out of sheer mischief, but not a breath was to be heard; I went feeling about the chamber, and with as little effect.

A horrible suspicion seized upon my fancy. There were two doors to the apartment, one opening upon the passage, the other into the boudoir; and both were locked as fast as doors could be. Where was the key my cousin Pattie turned when we entered the chamber together? It was gone. I discovered its absence, and looked round the chamber in astonishment and dismay.

At that moment some person in Mr. Periwinkle Smith's house, which was right opposite, entered a front chamber therein with a light, which streamed into the windows of Pattie's apartment with a lustre sufficient to make every object visible. My cousin Pattie was not to be seen! I looked under the bed, and into the bed; examined the presses, and peeped behind the chairs; but no cousin Pattie was to be found. She had locked *me* in the chamber, but not herself! Horror of horrors! she had played a trick upon me! she had jilted me! and—ay! there was no doubting it a moment longer—she had run off with my friend Tickle! "I'll show you how I serve fortune-hunters," said she—"lock him up in a closet—kick his heels till morning—eaten up by rats—shall hear yourself how I'll serve your rival Tickle." Death and destruction! and, after all, she has run away with him!— eloped in the very carriage I provided! married by the parson I engaged! decamped with the forty thousand I secured! and I—*I*, the unfortunate, jilted, cozened *I*—was the person left kicking my heels in a closet!

The idea filled me with phrensy; and the light from Mr. Periwinkle Smith's house being removed at the moment, I tumbled over a chair that lay in my way, and besides breaking my head and shin, woke up such a din in the house that the very servants in the kitchen bounced up in alarm, and screamed out for assistance.

"What's the matter, Pattie?" said my uncle Wilkins, turning the key which the faithless creature had left sticking in the outside of the door, and entering: "I say, Pattie, ods bobs, what's the—Lord bless us, cousin Ikey! is that you? what's the matter? what are you doing in Pattie's chamber?"

I answered my uncle Wilkins only by opening my mouth as wide as I could, and staring at him in anguish, horror, and despair.

"Where's Pattie?" said he, in alarm.

The question restored me to my faculties.

"Eloped," said I; "cheated me beyond all expression, and run off with my rival Jack Tickle."

"What a fool!" said my uncle, recovering his composure; "I'm sure I never opposed her."

"So much for not giving her to me!" said I.

"To you!" said my uncle.

"Uncle Wilkins," said I, "from this moment I shall cut your acquaintance. Pattie has jilted me so horribly you can't conceive, and has married Jack Tickle!"

"Well," said my uncle, "where's the harm? To be sure, and a'n't he as good now as worth ten thousand a year?"

"Not worth a cent!" said I, shaking my fists at the old gentleman—and then drumming on my own breast—"not worth a cent, and down in every tailor's books in town, except Snip's, who wouldn't trust him."

"Oh, you villain!" said my uncle Wilkins, "how you've cheated me!"

He ran down stairs, and I after him; he was bent upon pursuing his daughter—and so was I.

CHAPTER XXII.

IN WHICH SHEPPARD LEE FINDS THAT HE HAS MADE THE FORTUNE OF HIS FRIENDS, WITHOUT HAVING GREATLY ADVANTAGED HIS OWN.

As we reached the foot of the staircase, the house door opened, and in came my friend Tickle, dragged along—not by our dear and faithless Pattie, as we fondly supposed, but by the raging Nora Magee.

"Help, murder, help!" cried my friend Tickle.

"Och, murder, and twenty murders more upon ye, ye chatin crathur! and won't ye marry me?" cried Nora Magee.

My uncle Wilkins and myself rushed forward, lost in amazement, and separated the fury from her prey. "What is the matter?" cried both, "and where is Pattie?"

"The devil is the matter," cried Jack, panting and blowing; "and where Pattie is I know no more than you. I thought I was running away with her until I reached the squire's; and then I found I had this wild Indian under her cloak, who insisted I should marry her, or else—"

"Ay, ye murderin, faithless villain!" said Nora Magee, "I'll marry ye, or I'll have the breaches of promise and the damages out of ye! Och, but I have the law of ye; for didn't my Missus Pattie promise ye should marry me? I say, ye ugly-faced, hin-souled Tickle that they call ye, I have the law of ye, and I'll be married before the squire, or I'll have the breaches out of ye!"

"My breeches," said Jack, "you may have, and my coat and waistcoat too; for may I be hanged and quartered if I am not cheated out of my very skin."

"Where's my daughter Pattie?" said my uncle Wilkins. He looked at me, and I looked at him; it was plain my cousin Pattie had not run away with my friend Tickle.

Where could she be? I began to recover my spirits, when they were suddenly put to flight by a knock at the door, which being opened, a letter was thrown in, the messenger instantly taking to his heels, so that no one beheld him. It was a letter to my uncle Wilkins. He opened it and read the following words:—

DEAR PAPA AND HONOURED FATHER:

"This is to inform you that I don't like Mr. Tickle, and so can't marry him; and hope you will excuse me for following my own fancies, being now independent, as you have made me, for which I will remain your dutiful, loving daughter for life Give my love to cousin Dully, and tell him I consider him my best friend next to my dear papa and my dear husband— for, oh, papa, I'm really married, and going off travelling to-morrow.

"Hope you'll forgive us, papa, and shall ever love and pray for you, and rest your loving, dutiful children,

"*PATTIE* and DANNY BAKER."

"*Danny Baker!*" roared my uncle; "*Danny* Baker!" groaned I. The clodhopper had got her, and I had been only toiling in his service!

"Oh, you villain!" said my uncle Wilkins, "this is all your doings!"

"Sir," said I, "no hard words."

"You're a villain!" said my uncle; "you wanted to steal her yourself, and I a'n't sorry Danny Baker has choused you out of her; and for that reason I don't care if I forgive him. Yes, sir, I'll forgive Danny Baker; but for you, sir, I owe you a debt—"

"If you do," said Tickle, "pay him." But we took no notice of him—my uncle because he was enraged, and I because I was devoured by the greatness of my misfortune. In truth, the loss of my cousin Pattie was so unexpected, that it had astounded me out of my faculties. I was reduced to a mere automaton, conscious, indeed, of being in a horrible quandary, but incapable of seeing my way out of it; when I suddenly heard the voice, as I thought (or some one very like it), of my cousin Sammy at the door.

This roused me at once; I remembered that at this moment my Alicia was waiting for me, and I fell into a rapture.

"Uncle Wilkins," said I, "you may say what you please; Jack Tickle, you are a rascal; Nora Magee, you are a jade; but it is all one to I. D. Dawkins. I will marry my Miss Skinner."

As I spoke I looked upon the door, which, opening, disclosed a sight that petrified me, body and soul together. It was the apparition of my Alicia, in bridal array, leaning upon the arm of my cousin Sammy, and followed by a brace of youthful damsels decked in white flowers, all of whom stalked into the door with the solid step of flesh and blood, and advanced towards my uncle; my Alicia looking as silly and shame-faced as could be, while Sammy, on the contrary, held up his head and strutted like a turbaned Turk in the midst of his harem.

"What the deuse is all this?" said Jack Tickle. As for me, I could not speak a word, being a hundred fold more amazed than before. I looked at my Alicia, who, seeing me, began to blush, and bridle, and simper, and hold fast to Sammy's arm. As for Sammy, he looked not a whit the less Turkish, but marched up to his father as if charging him at the head of a regiment.

The old gentleman was as much astonished as myself, and at last cried out,

"Ods bobs! what's the matter, Sam? have you been running away, too?"

"No," said my cousin Sammy, "I reckon I'm not gone yet; but I've come to get ready: and first, dad, as in duty bound, let's have a bit of your blessing, if you've no objection, on me and my wife."

"Your wife!!!" said I, and said no more.

"Well," said my cousin Sammy, "I reckon I may say so; for you see, Dawkins, my boy, when I saw 'Lishy here, I liked her; and when July here came and told us as how you had run off with sister Pat Wilkins, why, then, said I, I may as well speak up for myself; and so, as the parson was ready, and 'Lishy dressed up to be married already, we made but short work of the courtship; and now, as the saying is, one and one *is* one: this here is my wife, for better and for worse, and I hope neither you nor father has any objection."

CHAPTER XXIII.

A CRISIS. SHEPPARD LEE IS REDUCED TO GREAT EXTREMITIES, AND TAKES REFUGE IN THE HOUSE OF MOURNING.

I never knew what my uncle Wilkins replied to the aforesaid speech, the longest I ever heard my cousin Sammy utter, nor do I know what reception he gave to the bride. I made but one jump to the front door, where my horror was consummated. My departure was greeted by an uproarious cry; but it proceeded from the street, not the house. I found myself among the Philistines, whom, an hour before, I had myself placed there in wait. I had forgotten the barbarians, which was natural enough, as they were my creditors; but they had not forgotten me. They hailed my appearance on the steps with some such yell of wrath and hunger as that with which the beasts of a menagerie express their joy at the appearance of their daily meal.

That cry was the finisher. I leaped from the steps and took to my heels, not, however, without leaving in the hands of my tailor one tail of the last coat he had made me; which was, I believe, the only payment I ever made him. My hat flew into the gutter; and that was perhaps recovered by its maker; in which case, it was doubtless brushed up and sold over again as a new one. I fled like the wind; my creditors followed me. The clatter of our footsteps, and the uproar of their interjections, threw the street into a tumult. Some persons yelled "murder!" and others cried "stop thief!" while the little boys, catching up the cry from a distance, screamed out "fire!" and ran to the nearest engine-house, to enjoy their evening amusement.

How long I ran, and whither, it is quite impossible for me to say. I recollect doubling two or three times, and diving into alleys, to throw my pursuers off the track. My efforts were, however, in vain; I found myself lodged at last in a vile alley, and hemmed in both on the front and rear. I made a leap at a garden gate, which I cleared; then running forward, and perceiving a back door in a house standing open, I rushed in, scarce knowing what I did.

I immediately discovered that I was in a sort of servants' hall, or anteroom to the kitchen, in which an old woman sat sleeping in an arm-chair. She was disturbed by the noise of my entrance, and I dreaded every moment to see her open her eyes, and by her shrieks draw my pursuers after me. I was afraid, however, to retreat, for, in the confusion of my mind, I thought I heard my tormentors rushing to and fro in the garden.

In this uncertainty, seeing a flight of stairs in one corner of the room, I darted up them, without reflecting a moment upon what might be the consequences. But what evil could happen to me more horrid than that I was fleeing? I might stumble into a lady's chamber and throw her into hysterics, or I might find myself at the bedside of some valiant personage, sleeping with a brace of pistols under his pillow, the contents of which he might transfer to my body. But such catastrophes had now lost their terrors: it was all one to I. D. Dawkins, as I had said to my uncle Wilkins. I could receive no addition to my woes, go whither and do whatsoever I might.

I rushed up the stairs, therefore, and entered a chamber, where a tallow candle, burning all on one side, stood flaring on a little table, among vials, gallipots, and other furniture of a sick chamber, throwing a dim and spectral light on a bed near to which it stood. I cast my eyes upon the bed, and perceived I had nothing to fear, either from timorous ladies or nervous gentlemen.

CHAPTER XXIV.

WHAT HAPPENED IN THE DEAD-CHAMBER.—THE DIRGE OF A WEALTHY PARENT.

Upon that couch lay the ghastly spectacle of a human corse, stiff and cold. It was that of an old man, and I thought at first that he slept; but, upon looking closer, I perceived that he had been dead for at least an hour; and it appeared as if he had died untended by friend or servant, for the bedclothes had been nearly tossed from the bed in his last convulsion, and now lay tumbled about his limbs and the floor, just as they had fallen. His features were greatly distorted, having an expression of rage upon them that was highly disagreeable to look on; yet I had a vague feeling that I had seen him before.

While I was wondering who he could be, I perceived a paper clutched in his right hand; and, taking it to the light, the secret was at once revealed.

It was a letter from my adorable Alicia to her father, dated that very evening, in which she gave him to understand, in the most romantic language in the world, that his opposition to her wishes in relation to her beloved Dawkins had broken her heart—that she could never think of marrying any one else (as if, indeed, the old gentleman ever wished her)—that she could not live without her Dawkins, and accordingly had made up her mind to fly with him afar from parental severity; and concluded by assuring him that "when he read those lines, penned by a grieved and determined, but still dutifully loving heart" (she said nothing of her fingers), "she would be in the arms of a lawful husband." There was appended a postscript, in which she expressed much contrition, hoped he would forgive her, and hinted that she would be of age in two months.

I looked at the old man again, and wondered I had not known him before. It was old Skinner, sure enough, and the secret of his death was readily explained. He had been sick before, and this elegant epistle had finished him—or rather the necessity, so romantically hinted at in the conclusion, of settling, two months thereafter, his guardian's account with her husband, had done his business. I did not suppose the wound in his parental feelings had done him much hurt; but there was more, perhaps, in that, than any one would have thought that knew the old miser.

And there he lay, then the owner of thousands and hundreds of thousands, with none to mourn him—nay, with not even a hand to smooth the bedrobe over his neglected body. He had squandered health, happiness, good name, and perhaps self-approbation, the true riches of man, in the pursuit of the lucre which cannot purchase back again one of these treasures; and notwithstanding which lucre he was now, and indeed had been at his death-hour, no better off than the beggar in his coffin of deal. He had heaped up gold for his children, that they might begrudge him the breath drawn in pain and infirmity, and rejoice in the moment of his death. He had—But why should I moralize over a subject worn just as threadbare as any other. The old fellow was a miser, and met the miser's fate. Nobody accused even his children of loving him; and while I stood by his side, I had a stronger proof of their regard than spoke in the neglected appearance of his deathbed. I had scarce entered the room before I heard, from some of the apartments below, the sounds of mirth and festivity.

They were not to be mistaken; it was plain that some persons were feasting and making merry in one of the old fellow's parlours; and I doubted not they were his two sons, Ralph and Abbot, both of whom had very bad characters, the latter in particular, who was a notorious profligate. They were young men of promise, I had heard; but the avarice of the parent had ruined them. Their education neglected from indifference, or a miserable spirit of parsimony, their minds and morals uncultivated,—the consciousness of their father's wealth and their own golden prospects at his decease stimulated them to excesses, which were perhaps rendered still more agreeable to their imaginations, and certainly more destructive to their weal, by the difficulty of indulging in them, resulting from the niggardliness of their father.

But the reign of denial was now over; the rattle and crash of glasses and vessels in the room below, the tumbling down of chairs and tables, with the sounds of singing, shouting, and laughter, proclaimed with what a lusty lyke-wake the abandoned sons were honouring the memory of their father—with what orgies of Bacchus they were celebrating their own deliverance from restraint. Suddenly the sound of the singing grew louder, as if some door between the revellers and the dead had been opened; and a moment after I perceived, from the increase and direction of the uproar, that the sots were ascending the stairs, and perhaps approaching the chamber of death.

An idea seized upon my mind. I was heartily sick of Mr. I. D. Dawkins's body, being ready at that moment to exchange it for a dog's, and I was incensed at the heartless and brutal rejoicings of the young Skinners. It occurred to me, if I could get my spirit into old Goldfist's body, I should avoid all dunning for the future, and give these two reprobate sons of his such a lesson as would last them to their dying day.

The idea came to me like a blaze of sunshine; I remembered in a moment the vast wealth of the deceased, and I pictured to my imagination the glorious use I should make of it. I had always hated and despised the old villain; but a sudden affection for him now seized upon my soul. I had a strong persuasion in me, resulting from my two former adventures, that I possessed the power of entering any human body which I found to my liking; and I resolved to exercise it, or, at the worst, to make proof of its existence, for a third time. Of the manner of exercising the power I knew but little; I remembered, however, that, on the former occasions, I had merely uttered a wish, and the transformation was instantly completed. I stepped up to the body, and chuckling with the idea of chousing the unnatural sons out of their expected inheritance, I said, "Old Goldfist, if you please, I wish to be in your body!"

In less than a second of time I found myself starting up from the bed, as if I had just been roused from sleep by the noise of some falling body, and exclaiming "What's that?"

I looked over the side of the bed, and saw the body of I. D. Dawkins lying on the floor on its face. The transformation was complete, and had been so instantaneous, that my spirit heard, through the organs of its new tenement, the downfall of its old. I felt a little bewildered, indeed posed, and remained upon my elbow staring about the room; and I may add, that I was more disconcerted by the bacchanalian voices now at the chamber door, than by any thing else.

The door opened, and the young Skinners entered; I shall remember them to my dying day; they were both royally drunk, and each armed with a candle, with which, scattering the tallow over the floor as they advanced, they came staggering and hiccoughing into the chamber.

"I say, bravo, dad, and no offence," said the foremost, "but don't feel so sorry as I ought; and here's Ralph a'n't sorry neither."

"Led us a devilish hard life of it," grumbled the other, "but shall have something done for his soul by the Catholics. I say, Abby, shall buy that black horse and the buggie."

"And a tombstone for dad," said the worthy Abbot, laying his candle upon the table, and striking an attitude like a dancing-master, which, however, he could not keep. "I say, Ralph," he went on, "it isn't right to say so, but don't you feel good? Three hundred thousand apiece, dammee! I say, Ralph, let us dance."

And the villains took hands, and attempted a *pas de deux*, as the theatre people have it; while the old woman, who had been sleeping below, and was roused by the fall of my late body, came running into the room, to see what was the matter. By this time the dogs had chassé'd up so nigh to the bed, that, for the first time, they laid their eyes upon the reanimated countenance of their father.

The effect was prodigious; the moment before their faces were all drunkenness and triumph—now they were all drunkenness and horror. The light of the candle held by Ralph flashed over my visage; but Abbot was the first to observe me resting on my elbow, and staring at him with looks of wrath and indignation.

"Lord love us, Ralph," said he, "dad's coming to!"

"Yes, you villains!" said I, "I am coming to; you unnatural, undutiful rascals, I *have* come to!"

They looked upon me, and upon one another, unutterably confounded, and I wondered myself that I did not laugh at them. Their confusion, however, only filled me with rage, and I railed at them with as much emphasis and sincerity as if I had been their father in earnest.

They dropped on their knees; but their rueful appearance only added to my fury. I stormed and I scolded, until, being quite exhausted with the effort, a film came over my eyes, and I fell back in a swoon.

BOOK IV.
CONTAINING ILLUSTRATIONS OF THE FOLLY OF BRINGING UP CHILDREN IN THE WAY THEY SHOULD GO, AND THE WISDOM OF MAKING A FORTUNE.

CHAPTER I.

THE PRIVATE HISTORY OF ABRAM SKINNER, THE SHAVER.

<hr>

My swoon was, I believe, of no great duration, and I awoke from it a new man, as well as an old one.

Yes, I was changed, and with a vengeance; and into such a miserable creature, that had I justly conceived what I was to become in entering old Goldfist's body, I doubt whether even the extremity in which I was placed would have forced me upon the transformation. I forgot that the title to Skinner's wealth was saddled with the conditions of age, infirmity, and a thousand others equally disagreeable. But I soon made the discovery, though it was some time before I discovered all.

The first inconvenience of the transformation which I felt was a thousand aches in my bones, a great disturbance in my inner man, and a general sense of feebleness and impotency, highly vexatious and tormenting. My eyesight was bad, my hearing indistinct, and, indeed, all my senses were more or less confused; my hand trembled when I lifted it to my face, my voice quavered while I spoke, and every effort to breath seemed to fill my lungs with coal-gas and ashes. In a word, I was a man of sixty years or more, with a constitution just breaking up, if not already broken.

My resuscitation produced a hubbub of no ordinary character. My sons— for, wonderful to be said, I *had* sons, and I soon felt as if they were in reality mine—were confounded, and so, doubtless, was Barbara, the housekeeper; to the latter of whom it was perhaps owing that I ever recovered from my swoon; for my two boys, overcome with horror and despair, rushed out of the house, and it was a week before I saw their faces again.

What added to the confusion was the discovery of my late body, lying on the floor, no one being at all able to account for its appearance. To this day, indeed, the thing remains a mystery among tailors and shop-keepers. It was pretty generally considered that the unfortunate I. D. Dawkins met his death by dunning, and I believe the coroner's jury returned a verdict accordingly; but how he made his way into the chamber of the usurer to give up the ghost, just at the moment the other was resuming it, was never known. Some supposed he had visited the old gentleman to borrow money, and had knocked his head against the bedpost in despair upon finding the lender past lending. Speculation was alive upon the subject for two full days, and was then buried in the young gentleman's grave, along with his body and his memory; for the memory of a dandy passeth away, unless recorded on the books of his tailor.

I was confined to my bed a week, suffering with a complication of disorders; for, though I possessed the power to reanimate a corpse, I had none to conjure away its diseases. In this period I had leisure to exchange all previous characteristics that might have clung to me, for those that more properly belonged to my new casing; and when I rose from my bed the transformation was in every particular complete. My soul had lost its identity; it had taken its shape from the mould it occupied; it was the counterpart of the soul of Abram Skinner.

My last act as I. D. Dawkins was to chuckle over the prospect of spending Abram Skinner's money; my first as Abram Skinner was to take care it should be spent neither by myself nor by any one else. The desire to enjoy myself had vanished; the thoughts of fine clothes, horses and carriages, and so on, entered my mind no more. The only idea that possessed me was, "What am I worth? how much more can I make myself worth?" and the first thing I did, when I could sit in a chair, was to ransack a certain iron chest that stood under my bed, containing my prototype's books of accounts, over which I gloated with the mingled anxiety and delight that had doubtless distinguished the studies of the true Goldfist.

I found myself rich beyond all my previously-formed expectations; and, glum and rigid as were now all my feelings, I think I should have danced around my chamber for joy, had not the first flourish of a leg introduced me to the pangs of rheumatism. I indulged my rapture, therefore, in a soberer way; and while awaiting the period of emancipation from my chamber, arranged a thousand plans for increasing my wealth.

My sons had deserted me, but I was not left entirely to solitude. I received divers visits from old fellows like myself, who, after growling out a variety of wonder and congratulation at my return to life, proceeded to counsel with me on subjects, the discussion of which speedily brought me to the knowledge of my new condition, where it had not been supplied by the iron chest and my instincts.

These persons formed a confraternity, of which it seems I, or rather my prototype, Abram Skinner, was a prominent member; and the objects of the association were to secure to each member the fruits of his ambition with as little danger and trouble as possible. We were a knot of what the censorious call stock-gamblers; and by working in common, and playing into each other's hands, without taking pains to acknowledge any connexion, we were pretty sure of our game.

It is astonishing how soon I entered into the spirit of my new character. On previous occasions, the adaption of soul to body was a work of time; but here it seemed the work of but a few hours. The cause was, however, simple; Abram Skinner was possessed of but one, or, at most, two characteristics, and with these I easily became familiar. The love of money was the ruling passion; and this, I honestly confess, came to me so naturally, that I was not conscious, while giving up my whole soul to it, of any change of character whatever. Before I left the house I was as busy shaving notes, receiving bonds, mortgages, and pledges (for Abram Skinner was a gambler of all work), and devising schemes for "cornering" and blowing high and low in the stock-market, as if I had been born to the business.

I found on my books the records of all imaginable operations, from the *mem.* of a thousand shares of the Moonlight Manufacturing Company, bought of A. B. on time, to the entry of "Mrs. C. D.'s silver spoons and pitcher, *purchased*" (Abram Skinner scorned all dealing on *pawns*, that being illegal to the unlicensed) "at such a sum, but redeemable at such another sum, which was generally at fifty per cent. advance, on a certain day, or— forfeit." Here was a memorandum of a note bought at half its value, there of a mortgage taken in form of a purchase; and in other places a thousand other forfeitures, such as marked the extent and universality of business, the skill, the forethought, and the success of Abram Skinner the shaver.

I have my compunctions when I think of the life I led that winter; for so long did I continue the life of a money-maker. But I entreat the reader to remember that I had got into Abram Skinner's body, and that the burden of my acts should be therefore laid upon his shoulders. A swearing gentleman once borrowed a Quaker's great-coat, with a promise not to dishonour it by any profanity while it was on his back; upon returning it to his friend, he was demanded if he had kept his promise. "Yes," said the man of interjections, with one of the most emphatic; "but it has kept me lying all the time." I never heard anybody doubt that the lying was the fault of the coat; and, in like manner, I hope that the reader will not hesitate to attribute all my actions, while in Abram Skinner's body, to Abram Skinner's body itself.

Besides my friends of the honest fraternity, I had other visitors before my infirmities permitted me to leave the house; and the dealings I had with them, besides enabling me to get my hand in, as the saying is, would afford the reader, if described, some insight into the excellences of my new character.

But I cannot pause over such pictures in detail. The rulers then over us, to please the poor, had got up a pressure in the money-market, whereby the poor were, as is usual in such cases, put under contribution by the rich. Such a pressure, however, may be said to please everybody, though it puts everybody in a passion. To the rich, who have money to lend, it is as great a season of jubilee as a rain-storm to ducks, or a high wind to the bristly herd in an apple-orchard, and they are in a passion because they fear it will be soon over; to the poor, who borrow their money at a higher rate than usual, it affords an opportunity to rail at the aristocracy, and the grinders of the poor; which is a pleasing recreation after a bad dinner. At such times Abram Skinner was a happy man, for he made money without the trouble of stirring from his house: every knock at the door was the signal of a god-send; every jerk at the bell was as the jingle of coming dollars and cents.

CHAPTER II.

SHEPPARD LEE'S FIRST HIT AT MONEY-MAKING.

It was at such a season that I entered the shaver's body. The knocks at my door were frequent, and the demands of my visiters to be brought into presence irresistible. What cared they for my pains and sickness?—they wanted money: what cared *I* for my pains and sickness? —I was anxious to make it. I ordered my house-keeper Barbara (for it seems I was such a niggard I had no other servant) to admit all well-dressed applicants; for I scorned to deal with any other.

The first person admitted was a woman, very good looking, but advanced in years. She kept a boarding-house, but, as Barbara informed me, had seen better days, having been the wife of a rich merchant, who failed, was absurd enough to keep his books so straight as to allow no opportunity for defrauding his creditors, surrendered up every cent of his property, and died a beggar, leaving a widow and six orphan daughters to lament his honesty.

She was in some little flurry and perturbation of spirits, but I spoke with a blandness that astonished myself, until I found that this was always my practice with a customer whom I was not tired of. This restored her to confidence and garrulity.

Her tale was soon told:—her boarders were all very fine gentlemen and ladies, and good pay; but the times were so hard, they were just at this moment compelled to pay with promises; with which coin her landlord was not so easily satisfied. She would not distress poor Mr. G., who owed her a hundred and fifty dollars, nor Mr. H., nor Mrs. I., who were all in a peck of trouble just then, but were well enough to do in the world—no, not she; she had heard I was so good as often to lend to people who wanted money for a few days, even when the banks would not, provided they were good and safe; and who was better and safer than she? With all her troubles, and the Lord he knew they were many and enough, she had always paid her debts, and she defied anybody to say the contrary: and so she hoped I would be so good as to oblige her with the small sum of two hundred-dollars, which, upon her honest word, she would pay as soon as she had the money.

To this eloquent suggestion I answered (and I doubt if the true Abram Skinner could have answered better) by lamenting her difficulties, and assuring her I was in as great trouble as herself, not having a cent at command that I could call my own (the iron chest told another story, and there were divers handsome hundreds placed to my credit in three or four different banks); nevertheless I had a little money belonging to a friend, which I thought I might make so free as to lend to one of her excellent character and standing; but that would be taking a great responsibility on my shoulders, &c. &c., in terms which the reader can easily imagine; and I concluded by hinting, that if she had any plate or other valuables to deposite as a security, it would save her the trouble of giving her note, and the inconvenience such an instrument might prove to her, if my friend's necessities should compel him to throw it into the market.

The widow, delighted with my frankness, and penetrated by my friendliness, ran home, and returned with a basket of chattels to the value of perhaps three hundred and fifty dollars.

"Very good," said I; "you shall have the money, though I should have to pay for it myself."

"Sure," said she, "but you are a good obliging man, and I shall be much beholden: and sure, but I thought all pawnbrokers had golden balls at their doors."

"Madam," said I, "thank your good fortune that I am *not* a pawnbroker. Had you gone to such a person you would have paid dear for your money, and perhaps lost your silver into the bargain. Now, supposing this silver to be worth three hundred dollars—"

"Three hundred lack-a-daisies!" said the old lady, "why, it cost more than four hundred dollars; for I remember the coffee-pot—"

"Yes, ma'am," said I; "that was the cost of making: I reckon the silver at about three hundred dollars, though that is a large allowance. Now, had you taken this to a pawnbroker, what do you think he would have loaned you on it?"

"To be sure, and I suppose; but I can't say."

"One hundred dollars, perhaps, if a moderate fellow," said I; "but *I* am another sort of man; I scorn to take any advantage of any one. Yes," said I, feeling warm and virtuous, "I scorn them there fellows that take advantage, and grind down the poor to the last mite. I, Mrs.—, hum, ha, Mrs.—"

"Mrs. Smith," said the old lady, eying me with admiration.

"*I*, Mrs. Smith, will treat you in another way; I will let you have what you want—the full two hundred dollars, for the space of thirty days, and charge you but twenty-five dollars for the favour."

"Sure," said Mrs. Smith, "and that's dear."

"On the contrary, madam," said I, "it is but twelve and a half per cent. a month, whereas money will often fetch fifteen."

"Will it, indeed?" said the foolish widow; "and sure but you must know better than myself. Well, then, Mr. Skinner, let me have the two hundred dollars, and you shall have the plate in pawn."

"No, ma'am," said I, "none but a pawnbroker can do that. A gentleman like myself does this sort of thing in another manner; for were I to receive this silver as a pawn, you might prosecute me for it in court, and make me pay a fine. The way we do is this; I *buy* the plate of you, for two hundred dollars, taking a receipt from you for that amount, and granting you, on my part, a written permission to purchase the same back again, this day month, for the sum of two hundred and twenty-five dollars."

"La!" said the old lady, "is that the way? But what if I should not get the money in a month?"

"Why, then," said I, with a look of benevolence, "why, then, I think I must give you a month longer."

"Sure and you are the best man in the world," said Mrs. Smith; "and you think my silver won't be in no danger? and you'll lock it up in some big iron chest? for thieves are quite thick already; and your paper to buy again will be just as good as a pawnbroker's certificate?"

I hastened to satisfy the old lady's mind on this and all other subjects. I then wrote out a receipt, which I caused her to subscribe, being a due acknowledgment on her part of having sold me certain specified articles of plate; after which I delivered her a paper, in which, without troubling myself to make any reference to the conveyance, I covenanted to sell her the same articles, at the price mentioned before, at the expiration of thirty days.

With this and the two hundred dollars which I now gave her, the foolish woman departed very well satisfied; and as for me, I actually rubbed my hands together with the delight of having made such a good bargain. I say again, old Skinner himself could not have managed the affair with greater address than myself; and, young as I was in his body, I felt as much satisfaction at having overreached a silly old woman, as ever a less avaricious man felt at deluding a young one. This was small game, to be sure, for a man who dabbled in stocks, and counted profits, not by dollars, but by hundreds and thousands; but, as I said before, Abram Skinner was a man of all work, who thought no gain small enough to be despised, and who cheated a single tatterdemalion with as much zeal as he would fleece a community.

The end of the bargain was this: in a month's time Mrs. Smith called on me again, but without money; whereupon I spoke to her with greater benevolence than before, assured her she need not be distressed, and renewed the engagement between us by adding twenty-five dollars (the interest upon the money advanced) to the sums specified in the conveyance and covenant; and the same amount I added at the expiration of the second month. And this course I intended to pursue for two months more, until the amount of interest should swell the purchase-money to three hundred dollars; after which I designed to close the bargain, and consider the silver fairly purchased.

If anybody supposes I treated the old woman ill—that I acted dishonestly, and even illegally, in the matter—all I have to say is, that I only did what Abram Skinner the shaver had done a thousand times before me, and what, I have no doubt, other worthy gentlemen of his tribe have done after me. He who rides with the devil must put up with his driving; and he who deals with his nephews must look for something warmer than burnt fingers.

The transaction with Mrs. Smith was a sample of divers others, begun and conducted on the same principles, though involving more momentous profits. The system of *forfeitures*, as practised by a skilful hand, is applicable to all species of property, and I practised it with great effect in the case of houses and lands, and the Lord knows what besides. The "pressure" continued long; and I think I should have made a handsome fortune in the course of the winter out of this single branch of my business alone, had not destiny arrested me in the midst of a prosperous career, and left the business to be settled by my administrators.

CHAPTER III.

REFLECTIONS ON STOCK-JOBBING AND OTHER MATTERS.

But this was but a branch, and a small one, of my profession. My noblest blows were struck at the community at large; and struck in that most magnificent of gambling-fields, the stock-market. My skill here—for I inherited all the sagacity and daring that had distinguished the original owner of my body—was such as to keep me at the head of that confraternity of which I have spoken before I was the very devil among the fancy stocks; and had the good luck to originate and conduct a stroke of *cornering*, by which no less than twenty young shop-keepers, who were ambitious to be seen on 'change and in brokers' offices, and to dare that achievement of audacity, *selling on time*, were smashed like coal-candlesticks, and half as many wiser and richer desperadoes were driven to the verge of ruin.

My chief strength, indeed, was shown in the management of small stocks, and especially those that were good for nothing, and more especially still in southern mining-companies. It was here that we of the Clipping Club, as the members of the fraternity delighted to call themselves, found our fairest opportunity to prey upon those passions of cupidity and terror which lay the ignorant at the mercy of the knowing. No one knew better than myself how to get up or depress such a stock. I knew how many ignorant widows, poor parsons, infirm artisans, and other needy persons were to be cajoled, by the prospect of handsome and increasing dividends, to invest their petty savings when it could be done at small premiums; and I knew how easily the terror of loss could drive them out of their investments. To say the truth, the principal business of myself and my brother clippers was to bob for such minnows; and it is incredible how they bite, though it is only to be bitten. A few words scattered at random, and still fewer uttered in confidence, were enough to send shoals of these unlucky creatures to swallow what we thought proper to sell; and a few doubts and long faces, added to the throwing away at low prices of a *few* dozen shares, sufficed to convert the trembling holders into sellers, whenever we deemed it advisable to buy. In this way I have known a pet stock to be tossed up and down like a ball, while every ascent and downfall served the purpose of filling the pockets of the fraternity and emptying those of the victims.

In such occupations as these passed three months of my existence, and, sinner that I am, I thought that they passed very honestly. The spirit of Abram Skinner had left such a taint of rascality in his body, that my own was thoroughly imbued with it; from which I infer that a man's body is like a barrel, which, if you salt fish in it once, will make fish of every thing you put into it afterward. A grain of lying or thieving, or any such spicy propensity, infused into the youthful breast by a tender parent, will give a scent to the spirit for life; and as this is a fact, I recommend parents to take no notice of it,—not supposing parents will take advice, except by contraries. The passion of Abram Skinner destroyed every trait that had belonged to Sheppard Lee; and as for those I had taken from John H. Higginson and I. D. Dawkins, they were lost in like manner. I was Abram Skinner, and nothing but Abram Skinner. I scarce remembered that I had ever been any thing else. I am free now to confess, what I was not so certain of then, though I had my doubts on the matter at times,—namely, that in labouring so hard after lucre, I was only striving to sell my soul to the greatest advantage.

Idleness is said to be the root of all evil. The root of *much* evil I never doubted it was. But my experience in the body of Abram Skinner has convinced me, that the industry to which a man is goaded by the love of money is the root of much greater evil,—of a bigger *upas*, indeed, than ever sprung from the bed of the sluggard. The idler may betake him to the bottle, as the idler usually does, and then lapse into a reprobate, which is a common consequence; but, at the worst, his crimes are committed at the expense of individuals. The man of avarice drinks out of his purse, which intoxicates quite as deeply as the bowl, makes war upon communities, preys legally upon his neighbour's pocket, and just as legally consigns his neighbour's children to want and beggary, from which it appears that he is a drunkard, thief, and murderer, just as naturally as the idler. The latter, by indulging his propensity, loses his character; the former, by indulging his, loses all those generous sentiments and feelings, the sense of honour and instinct of integrity, upon which character should be founded. The man who enriches himself by extracting wealth from the soil and the bowels of the earth, or by the practice of any art or business which supplies the necessaries of life, or ministers to the convenience of society, makes his money virtuously, and deserves to enjoy it in honour; but he who gains a fortune by the mere gambling legerdemain of speculation, by turning his neighbour's pockets wrong side out, is—not so much of a Christian as he supposes. My honest opinion, formed after much reflection and experience, is, that bulls and bears are as little likely to go to heaven as any other animals.

In regard to myself, I am as free to confess, that my course of life while in Abram Skinner's body was deserving of all reprobation. I hope that the acts I then committed may be laid to old Skinner's door; but, for fear of a mistake, I have endeavoured to repent them, as being sins of my own committing: and this course I recommend to all those good folks who are persuaded their peccadilloes are the fault of others, and for the same reason,—namely, lest they should be mistaken. I confess also that I had my doubts, even at the time of committing them, of the righteousness of my acts, and that I sometimes had bad dreams: but the fury of avarice stilled the pangs of conscience, as the fury of wrath and battle stills those of the wounded soldier. Having made these admissions, I will now betake me to my story.

END OF VOL. I

www.ingramcontent.com/pod-product-compliance
Lightning Source LLC
Chambersburg PA
CBHW031433270326
41930CB00007B/682